"Why are y[ou] Jake?" Amber asked wary[ly]

"You know me. I hear of something, it intrigues me, I follow it to the bitter end—"

"It's more than that."

"I believe strongly in justice, Amber. And I have a personal interest in this. There's a chance that you're Vincente St. Honoré's daughter. You ought to know, one way or the other. You and your child could stand to inherit his plantation and I want to help you find out the truth."

"That's kind of you," she said gratefully. "But I'm not sure I want to know. I thought when we were married I'd have a quieter life. It seems I'm being flung back into the maelstrom."

"I'll be with you every step of the way."

"Thank you, Jake. You're being very kind to me again," she said. And she pleaded silently, *Please let me feel I can put my trust in him, and let it be justified!*

Jake lightly stroked her furrowed brow till the lines were ironed out. "I don't think we'll forget our wedding day in a hurry!" he said ruefully, and they both laughed.

Dear Reader,

Sara Wood's colorful new trilogy is full of family intrigue, secrets, lies and, of course—love. It involves the St. Honoré family, which has a reputation second to none in St. Lucia. Mandy, Ginny and Amber are drawn into this notorious family and the secrets of its past. Each of these intrepid heroines is looking for love and each of them will find it—but only where they least expect it!

In *White Lies* (#1910), Mandy Cook is desperate to find her father, and perhaps Vincente St. Honoré can help her. If she can ever find him! For first she must wrest herself from the arms of his commanding and charismatic son—Pascal.

In *Scarlet Lady* (#1916), Ginny McKenzie is a successful fashion model, but her worst nightmares are confirmed as she is wrongly branded a scarlet lady by the press and loses her husband, the Hon. Leo Brandon, as a result. It is only when, two years later, she decides to search for love elsewhere that Ginny is reunited in St. Lucia with the man she has always loved—Leo! The question is, why is he there?

In *Amber's Wedding*, the final book in the trilogy, Amber Fraser has just married Jake Cavendish, not for love but for convenience, companionship and to secure a father for her unborn child. On their wedding day Jake reveals to Amber a secret that will change her life. A secret that will finally reveal the truth about the St. Honoré family. They honeymoon in St. Lucia, where love appears to blossom after all—until Amber discovers Jake's real motive for marrying her.

Happy reading!

The Editor

SARA WOOD

Amber's Wedding

Harlequin Books

TORONTO • NEW YORK • LONDON
AMSTERDAM • PARIS • SYDNEY • HAMBURG
STOCKHOLM • ATHENS • TOKYO • MILAN
MADRID • WARSAW • BUDAPEST • AUCKLAND

ISBN 0-373-11922-4

AMBER'S WEDDING

First North American Publication 1997.

Copyright © 1996 by Sara Wood.

This edition published by arrangement with Harlequin Books S.A.

® and TM are trademarks of the publisher. Trademarks indicated with ® are registered in the United States Patent and Trademark Office, the Canadian Trade Marks Office and in other countries.

Printed in U.S.A.

With my grateful thanks to Mrs. Joan Devaux,
Gary Devaux, Maria Monplaisir
and all at Anse Chastanet

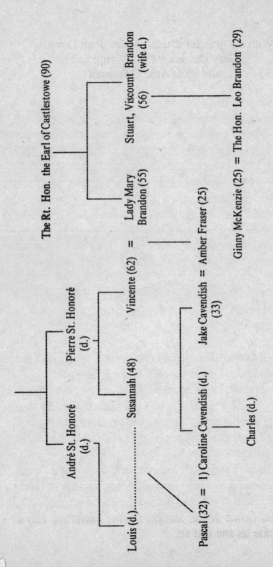

The Rt. Hon. the Earl of Castlestowe (90)

Lady Mary Brandon (55)

Stuart, Viscount Brandon (56) (wife d.)

Ginny McKenzie (25) = The Hon. Leo Brandon (29)

Vincente (62) =

Amber Fraser (25)

André St. Honoré (d.)

Pierre St. Honoré (d.)

Susannah (48)

Jake Cavendish = Amber Fraser (25) (33)

Louis (d.)

Pascal (32) = 1) Caroline Cavendish (d.)

Charles (d.)

2) Mandy Cook (25)

CHAPTER ONE

'DID you say...the Caribbean?'

Astonished, Amber whirled around so fast that her gossamer bridal veil flew across her face, obscuring her view for a moment. Impatiently she pushed it back and thrust her heavy mass of red-gold hair off her bare shoulders for good measure. 'You're kidding me!' she accused her old friend.

Leo leaned against a pillar of the minstrels' gallery and grinned. 'Well! I've got your attention at last! Here I am, telling you that I'm setting up home in St Lucia,' he protested, 'and all you can do is drool over your new husband!'

'Jake?' Her surprise wiped out Leo's startling news. Amber frowned. Had she been drooling? How odd! 'I wasn't...surely?'

'Constantly!'

'I didn't know!' She recovered herself and managed to look bashful. 'I'd be an odd bride if I didn't.'

And an odd bride she most definitely was! It was more than likely that her marriage to Jake was the oddest that had ever taken place in Castlestowe's small kirk. A marriage of convenience. No sex, no emotional hassle, only a warm affection. Perfect.

She had no particular feelings for Jake other than those of friendship. That was why her apparent fascination for him baffled her. Before she could stop herself, she glanced down at the throng below, suffering Leo's fond chuckle as she did so.

7

Guests in bright tartans and colourful ballgowns filled Castlestowe Castle's baronial hall. Jake's tall, athletic figure in a black dinner jacket stood out amongst them. But then he would be very striking in any crowd.

Amber studied his lampblack, Byronic curls and extraordinarily arresting face. Tonight he seemed to glow with joy, his dark eyes alight with the kind of shining happiness of any blissful groom. But he wasn't a blissful groom. So why was he ecstatic?

She frowned and tried to forget the misgivings she'd had ever since Jake had said, 'I do,' and smiled at her with disarmingly warm affection. When she'd returned the smile, she'd thought for a moment that there had been a curl of desire on his eloquent mouth. And she wanted friendship. Unfortunately he *was* sexy. He *was* a man—and she didn't have much faith in men's promises when their hormones were involved.

'I suppose Jake must seem like a different person to you now he's more conventionally dressed. A DJ isn't the same as a bush shirt, flak jacket and decorative dust,' Leo said helpfully.

Yes. That was why she'd found Jake intriguing—the sartorial contrast. Mystery solved! 'Elegant, isn't he? I never knew he could look so civilised!' she agreed with a light laugh.

Almost civilised, but not quite, she mused. There was an element of Jake that scared her a little. It was partly the fact that he risked his life a mite too often, partly something she couldn't define. Behind the charm and the laid-back manner, she sensed something darker. There was a whole bunch of secrets in those near-black, fathomless eyes.

Several times during their acquaintance in the past when she'd been chatting animatedly to him about her family back home he'd made an abrupt excuse and left, as if her joy had hurt him somehow. She'd learnt to throttle back on the happy-family stories, sensing that he had problems that he did not wish to share. No one had ever got close to Jake or broken the seal over his heart. And it was clear that he was a fascinating challenge to women.

They'd known one another for years, off and on—he in his capacity working for Reuters, the most highly respected news agency in the world, she as a fieldworker for Unite, the organisation that brought lost refugee children back to their parents. They'd met in Bucharest, bumped into one another in Sarajevo and Rwanda and recently on another African posting.

And every time he'd eased his lithe body out of a Jeep on his habitual rounds of the refugee camps he'd turned the women workers' heads with his devastating charm, his sword-blade cheekbones and wickedly dancing eyes. The adjective most commonly used about Jake was stunning. Women found him easy to get on with—a beguiling man with a core of steel.

A twinge of anxiety troubled her chocolate-brown eyes. That sexy manner had been the only thing about him that had made her hesitate when they'd arranged the marriage. Only the warmth she felt for him and his assurance that he understood how she felt had persuaded her to agree. Jake knew how she felt about sex— and why.

Firmly she told herself that she was worrying unnecessarily about Jake. He'd been good to her. Her face softened with admiration for the sophisticated man who could lift the camp-fire conversation with his wit and humour one night and disappear into hostile territory the next, armed with only a notebook and a change of underwear. A real toughie beneath that deceptive, sensitive-poet appearance.

'He's rather...deliciously *dissolute*-looking, Amber!' one of her old university friends had gleefully said during the wedding reception—and there had been regret in her friend's tone that Jake hadn't come *her* way first.

But Amber knew that for the last ten years Jake had been busy roaming around the world, actively seeking out news stories, and he didn't have time for meaningful relationships or emotional commitment.

And she'd married him. Did that make her wise or foolish?

'You are...happy?' Leo queried gently. 'Once or twice today you've seemed rather brittle.'

She threw back her head and laughed. To her ears there was a slight tinge of hysteria about it so she toned it down. 'This is my wedding day!' she chided gently. 'And only two weeks ago Jake and I were in Africa. It was tough in the camp. I'm adjusting to being home—and being a married woman!'

'It's been a bit of a rush job.' Leo chuckled. 'If people didn't know you better, they'd have been checking your waistline!'

'Good grief!' she squawked, fiercely quelling her overwhelming desire to press her hand to her stomach. Her child lay there. And it wasn't Jake's. A faint sensation of nausea rose to her throat. 'My reputation as a vestal virgin would be shot to pieces, wouldn't it?' she managed to joke.

Trembling, she rested her shaking hands on the back of a heavily carved chair, longing to sink into it. And with the truth making her stomach knot she hastily changed the subject before her conscience made her confess.

'Now, Leo! About this Caribbean plantation—'

'Yes—not only am I going to live there with Ginny, but we're getting married again!' he said happily.

Amber grasped his hand in delight. He'd been like a bear with a sore head after his divorce from Ginny. '*Wonderful!* I'm glad for you. But...'

Her face fell as she thought of Leo's father. Stuart, Viscount Brandon was also her own dearly loved godfather and, since her parents were dead, he had given her the wedding as his present to her.

'How can you leave?' she continued reproachfully. 'You run the estate. You know every contour, every blade of grass, every outcrop of granite. The land, the village, the castle... they're life and breath to you, just as they are to me. You stand to inherit Castlestowe. *I* love it with all my heart—and I'm only a gillie's daughter,' she said, proud that her family had been servants to the Brandons for generations. 'I swear I'd *never* leave it—'

'But I love Ginny more,' he told her softly.

The plain statement brought her up with a jolt. It was so sweetly said, so deeply meant. Why she should feel envious she didn't know. After her recent disastrous affair with Enzo, she'd decided that entrusting her heart to a man was too great a risk. A loveless marriage was far more sensible. It suited her and it suited Jake...

Jake! Every time she blinked she seemed to be thinking about him! They were supposed to operate independently, not go around tied up together in thought, word and deed!

Amber carefully avoided looking at the black-clad figure in the centre of the room and gazed ardently around the great baronial hall of the fairy-tale castle. The room blazed richly with the warm golden light of hundreds of giant candles carefully set in the massive chandeliers. Ancient, age-tattered banners flew from the medieval niches, proudly representing long-forgotten battles fought by the Brandon family, and the hall was filled with lively music and the swirl of kilts as guests flung themselves wholeheartedly into a vigorous reel.

Gillies, tenants, farmers, tradespeople, journalists, Members of Parliament, the cream of Scottish society... All thronged the huge, beamed hall, filling it with chatter, laughter and movement.

It made her heart ache to be here. She loved Castlestowe. Loved the way it sat, solid and confident, on the windswept crag, its turrets and drawbridge quite magical, amidst acres of feudal moorland, sky that went on for ever and white virgin beaches. Nothing in this world could touch it!

She smiled at the extent of her own fervour. 'Ginny's always hated it here. She really is picky!'

Leo laughed at her impassioned face and surprised her with a warm hug. 'Sweetheart,' he said, 'to Ginny this place is cold, wet and unwelcoming. I love Ginny. I want her to be happy, as Jake wants *you* to be happy. He's agreed to make his base here because he loves *you*, hasn't he? Same difference.'

Jake hadn't agreed—that was the trouble. He'd said he'd see how he felt about living in Scotland and she'd silently vowed to make him love it.

'Nothing could tear me away from Castlestowe,' she said determinedly. 'Nothing!'

Still enclosed in Leo's arms, Amber felt the hairs on her neck rise. Jerking her head around to look at the hall below, she saw Jake's face lifted to them and met the full force of his eyes. She felt herself freeze. He looked . . . angry.

Her entire body tensed with an irrational fear. Her chest tightened so disturbingly that she had to draw in a series of quick little breaths to ease her straining lungs as she remained within the circle of Leo's arms and Jake slowly turned his dark eyes to Leo.

'Hell! That's a look and a half!' muttered Leo in awe.

'Oh, he's a pussy-cat really!' she declared unconvincingly, flapping her hand in a cheerful wave to Jake, to cover up her unnerving sense of foreboding.

'I think his claws are out.' Leo pushed her back a little. 'Your husband's jealous. I think you'd better make it clear what our relationship is!'

'*Jealous?*' Amber went very still, her eyes slanting again to where Jake stood. And then she understood. It was a necessary part of the act, she supposed, to be annoyed at seeing your bride in another man's arms. 'But of course he is!' she said lightly, playing along with the pretence. 'So he should be.'

No one could know how safe Jake's real lack of interest had made her feel. Free from any complicated emotions towards him, she'd been able to relax with him. Thankfully, she and Jake wanted the same thing: to remain good friends and stay mercifully immune from the dangers of love.

Love was frightening. It tore out your heart and threw it at someone's feet where it lay pumping out your life's blood. It left you open to having that raw heart trampled on without regard to your dignity or pride. Love was like standing on a greasy pole with a tiger pit below.

Thankfully her brief, destructive affair was over. Her marriage to Jake would ensure that she never experienced such misery again.

She smiled at Jake in a sudden rush of gratitude. He lifted a disapproving eyebrow in Leo's direction then beckoned her with an authoritative finger to come down to the hall.

Smiling, she lifted her hand and, splaying out her fingers, mouthed, 'Five minutes!'

Jake frowned and turned away. His heavy lids were lowered, his lashes making shadowed smudges on his sabre-cut cheekbones. She watched as his head bent and he murmured something urgently to the women around him, his mouth taking on a ravishingly wicked curl as he did so.

'You can't take your eyes off him, can you?' chuckled Leo.

'Yes! Oh, OK, *no*! He's...very compelling!' she answered reluctantly. And felt worried that it seemed to be true. Why was that? she wondered, feeling a sensation as if a hundred butterflies were dancing on her skin. Butterflies with hot feet; her body tingled with warmth and she fanned her face with her hand. 'Heavens, isn't it hot?'

'Not particularly,' said Leo. 'But I know the feeling.'

She hardly heard. Her eyes were glued to Jake as he strode purposefully across the dance floor towards the door that led to the servants' quarters.

Leo touched her arm gently. 'Amber, you understand why I'm leaving, don't you? I can't leave Ginny in her hour of need. Places and possessions are nothing to me. Only Ginny. You'd give up everything for Jake, wouldn't you?'

She managed a wan smile. 'Are you kidding?'

But she wouldn't. To her there was only one place to live in the world. It didn't matter to Jake where they lived. He could continue working around the world as a war correspondent while she stayed in Castlestowe, with people she'd known all her life around her.

'I'll have children,' said Leo, breaking in on her thoughts. 'One of them might love the idea of taking over Castlestowe on my behalf. Father's reconciled to that idea. He's looking forward to grandchildren. And...maybe you and Jake will come to visit us some time?' He grinned mischievously. 'Compare children, maybe?'

He knew! she thought in horror, and then saw that he was laughing at her startled expression. Somehow she again managed not to touch her stomach in a protective gesture. Somehow she stretched her lips into a smile.

'Whoa, there! Steady! I'm only just married,' she protested, quelling the nausea that threatened her composure.

Leo gave her a goodbye hug and slipped away. Suddenly exhausted, she sat down on a tapestry-covered chair which was tucked away out of sight of the revellers below. It was then that her hand instinctively crept to where her baby lay.

She didn't even know how she felt about the baby. There'd been no time to register anything other than shock and then a shy joy and then... Then she'd told its father—Enzo, the handsome UN captain who had been responsible for the African enclave where she'd been working.

'It's all right,' he'd told her some two months or so earlier, when protective supplies had run out. 'I'll be careful, I promise. I love you. I need you... Please, Amber! *Please...*'

She'd denied him; he'd insisted. And stupidly she'd let him persuade her because he'd swamped her in passionate, emotional blackmail, and life out there was so tough that you took your pleasure with a desperation that would be unthinkable under more normal circumstances.

Their relationship had cooled the next morning because she'd felt used. Her white teeth drove deep into her full lower lip. Love, he'd said! It had been lust, though she'd been too naïve and innocent to recognise it as such. And Enzo had been annoyed when she'd hesitantly told him that she was pregnant.

'What can I do about it? I'm married,' he'd said with a shrug, unaware that Amber had frozen with the shock.

Then he'd gone on to say that their six-month affair had been fun, wonderful, sensual and he adored her, of course; she was the best lay he'd ever had . . . but nothing else.

She felt weak at the memory. The best lay. Amber drew in a shuddering breath as the humiliation hit her anew. Enzo had vanished, leaving her incapable of work. Even her team leader, Mary Smith, had been unable to console her.

Then Jake had stepped in, acting with typical thoughtfulness and sensitivity. He'd come across her huddled body in the Jeep that Enzo had used and he'd talked to her for ages. While she'd sobbed her heart out, his soothing, velvety voice had persisted, relentlessly describing some of the children waiting for a trace on their parents, making them real to her by his accurate observations—one child's crooked smile, another's saucy eyes, the family of four looked after by the eldest—a child of nine . . .

Slowly he'd brought her back to the world again. But this time she'd met it and her obligations without any love in her heart. And with a child secretly growing in her body.

Her face flamed with the shame. 'Enzo! Oh, *Enzo!*' she groaned in misery.

There was a sharp intake of breath behind her and she jerked her head around, releasing a flurry of creamy petals from the roses which secured her floating veil. Jake! she registered, ignoring the fall of velvety petals onto her breasts. And her tearful eyes widened. He was tense with anger.

'What's the matter?' she asked in confusion.

'Surely you know?'

Her heart thudded at the passion shaking his voice.
He remained in the dark shadows of the stone arch which
led to the stairs and speculatively examined the bright
flame of her hair in a way that suggested he found her
beautiful. Slowly his gaze drifted over her gleaming,
satiny shoulders and she stiffened, hypnotised by his
brooding expression. And she felt alarmed at the implications of the undeniably sexual inspection.

Short of breath suddenly, she inhaled, lifting her
breasts where the velvet petals lay sprinkled in romantic
abandon. Without realising it, she had innocently invited his disturbing gaze, because a few of the petals
wafted into the deep *décolleté* neckline.

'I—'

'Mmm?'

There was a perturbing softness to his mouth, a strange
yet dangerous glow in his eyes that made her catch her
breath again. Her intense awareness of his sensuality was
bewildering. She'd never felt like this about him before.
Perhaps he'd kept it from her. Perhaps he'd deliberately
waited till... Her teeth drove briefly into her lower lip,
stopping her fancies, and she started again.

'I need a moment, Jake,' she said, strangely croaky.
Her fingers twined tightly around one other as if they
needed to hold onto something. 'I'm a bit chewed
up—'

'So I heard.' His drawl vibrated with a controlled
anger. 'I think you owe me a few explanations. Shall we
start with your feelings for Enzo?'

For a moment she didn't know what he was talking
about, and then she remembered that she'd been whispering her ex-lover's name with a deceptively suspicious
sadness.

Licking her dry lips, she said defensively, 'I'm not
upset because of... him—'

'No? It sounded as if you were. You have to forget him. He's not worth your time,' Jake retorted testily.

Embarrassment washed over her like a hot wave. 'I *am* trying to forget it all. I was just going over the past...regretting my mistakes, if you must know. I need—'

'I know what you need. A shoulder, a protector, a father to your child.'

The liquid of his voice disturbed her. Amber nodded, gaining time to steady herself. 'Yes, I married you because I needed a husband,' she admitted. 'Don't think I'm regretting our marriage—'

'You said it was a feudal community.' Jake's dark eyes studied her carefully. 'Puritanical. That you'd never be able to live here as the mother of an illegitimate child—'

'That wasn't the only reason I agreed to marry you.'

'Oh?' he enquired softly. 'Something else, then?'

She'd been about to mention their friendship, the close bond she thought they could have. But something faintly suggestive in his tone prevented her. She stuck to the facts instead.

'We both want the convenience of a marriage without love, don't we?' she asked, a little unevenly.

To be honest, it wasn't really what she'd expected. Once, she'd believed that marriage stood for love and commitment. But circumstances meant that she'd had to make a choice under pressure.

There had been cholera in the camp. The doctor there who'd examined her and confirmed her pregnancy had insisted that she return home at once. She'd known that it would only be a little while before everyone in Castlestowe knew of her shame, and that she might have to leave her beloved home. She couldn't have borne that. So Jake had offered her a solution.

'No love, no ties. What more could a confirmed bachelor desire?' he drawled now, his dark lashes veiling his eyes. Amber wondered what he was hiding. Nervously, she fiddled with her neckline. Jake cleared his throat and continued.

'I've always said that a wife and children would be millstones around the neck of a war correspondent like me,' he murmured. 'A man would be a fool to walk into a danger zone and risk snipers' bullets if he had a woman and child he loved at home.'

'Whereas I won't make any difference to the way you feel, will I? And don't worry, I know that your nomadic existence has made you more independent than most and you balk at restrictions and routine. I won't tie you down.'

'I'm relieved.' Jake gave her a crooked smile. 'If I'm to have a wife, I'd prefer to be her friend. Friends give one another space. I know you want very little from me, and that suits me fine. I can't stand women who cling. Our arrangement is ideal.'

'Because you don't need to pretend you love me.'

His mouth took on a wry twist. 'I don't need to pretend that, no,' he said huskily.

Amber wondered what had happened to make Jake so detached. He'd hinted of a broken heart—one that would never mend. It explained why he always kept a part of himself back. Hopefully, he'd learn to trust her in time and share some of his past with her. As to the future...

Suddenly she thought of him lying dead somewhere abroad and she went pale. 'You'll still risk your life, I suppose,' she said quietly.

'It's my job. My job *is* my life. I feel a passionate need to tell the world what is happening out there, to report the truth and help to prevent injustice.' He gave a short laugh and met her eyes again. 'I'm very hot on injustice, Amber.'

She smiled. 'I admire that,' she said earnestly. 'It colours everything you do. Your parents must be very proud of you.'

'Less proud of my professional achievements than they are to hear I'm married at last,' he said ruefully.

She laughed with him. His parents had been obsessed with his bachelor state. Occasionally, after ringing their home in Kenya, he'd met her in the camp mess tent and exasperatedly confided that all they could ask was whether he'd found a nice girl yet.

'The heat would have been off you if you'd had brothers or sisters,' she said sympathetically.

He shrugged, a hard line to his mouth. 'It's off now.'

'I'm sorry your parents couldn't come.'

'Only malaria could have kept Father away,' Jake said wryly. 'Prepare yourself for when we tell them you're pregnant. My mother will start knitting...and Father will see some purpose to his life again.' His expression became very serious. 'Amber, I love them both. They've had a rough time. A lot of troubles which I'll tell you about one day. I'd like them to be happy.'

Amber could see that his affection was genuine. It was something she could relate to. A man who loved his parents and cared so much for their welfare would make a good husband.

A sudden, sharp heat invaded her stomach. Dismayed, she closed her eyes tightly, willing herself not to be sick, here, in front of Jake. On her wedding day! The ghastliness of the situation made her wince.

'You're ill?' He didn't seem to miss anything. 'You look very pale.'

She heard him move and felt him come close, knowing that he must have knelt and was inches from her by the sudden pressure of his cool fingers pressing lightly on her temples. Her lids flew open and she met his black-molasses gaze in consternation because he was far too near for comfort.

'Please don't touch me! I'll be OK!' she lied. 'Leave me alone for a while!' she begged, her voice rising a betraying octave.

'I can hardly abandon you when you look so sick. What's wrong?' he asked with a frown, beginning to brush the petals from her bare shoulders.

She stiffened. The light touch of his fingers was strange, almost in the form of a warm caress. 'Don't!' she repeated sharply. The sickness surged up again and she swallowed hastily before saying, 'Nothing's wrong. I—'

'Don't lie. There is a problem. Tell me,' he ordered.

'All *right*!' Denying her nausea in the hope that mind could conquer matter, she put aside the fear that Jake wasn't as indifferent as she'd first imagined and concentrated on her misery at losing Leo. 'I feel depressed because Leo's left Castlestowe,' she mumbled, and he gave a quick intake of breath.

'Ah.' He looked annoyed again. 'We come to Leo.'

Sadly she gazed at Jake's grim face. 'He and Ginny are getting married again,' she explained. 'They're going to live in St Lucia!'

With great deliberation, Jake unfolded his long limbs and stood up. 'Just as well,' he observed with crisp finality.

'How can you say that?' Amber objected, craning her neck upwards. 'Stuart will be devastated! Leo will be living miles and miles away from his father—'

'It's only a nine-hour flight,' Jake pointed out drily. 'Besides, you told me they've never been close. In fact,

I'd say that Stuart Brandon loves you more than he loves his son. Don't look so shocked! It's true.'

'Well, Leo was brought up by nannies and sent to boarding-school,' she said quickly.

'Mmm.' Jake paused and considered her thoughtfully, as if that wasn't the whole explanation. 'Whereas you, a godchild, have been loved by Stuart and treated like an honorary daughter ever since you were born. Look at this wedding reception he's provided for you!'

'He's been very good to me,' she admitted.

'Surprisingly so.'

'You don't understand.' Amber watched him fold his arms in a disturbingly challenging way. 'The Brandons treat the people who work for them like family. My father grew up with Stuart. They had a mutual respect for one another. And, as you know, Stuart took a shine to me when I was little.'

'There's no denying that. You and Castlestowe are the great loves of Stuart's life,' said Jake shrewdly. 'I'm sure he won't miss Leo too much—nor will he mind running the estate. I think he'll enjoy striding over the moors in tweeds and brogues. He'll prefer that to living in London as a Member of Parliament and wearing city suits and breathing city air. He doesn't strike me as the sort to enjoy Westminster life.'

'Maybe you're right,' Amber conceded, knowing that her godfather hated London and only stayed to press Scotland's causes. 'I'm worried about Leo's grandfather, though. He won't be pleased at all.'

She saw Jake's nod of acknowledgement. They'd visited the bedridden Earl a few times, in his suite at the castle.

'He's coped with tragedy before. Odd that he thought you resembled his late wife,' Jake mused idly.

It was true. The portrait in the old earl's bedroom bore a remarkable likeness to her: a tall, stately woman with fiery hair and a broad, earthy face. But she was Amber Fraser, the daughter of Angus Fraser, a gillie at Castlestowe like all his ancestors before him. And the Brandons were bred-in-the-bone aristocrats.

'We're the same Scottish type,' she said, dismissing the matter. 'Well, when the old Earl dies, Stuart will be the next Earl of Castlestowe—and after him Leo will inherit the title. He should stay.' Her face fell. Without Leo's friendship, she'd be lost.

Jake frowned. 'He means a lot to you, doesn't he?'

'Yes!' she replied, her eyes soft with tears.

He began to stride up and down the gallery as if he felt confined, then came to a brief halt in front of her. 'Now he's gone, at least I won't have to worry about leaving you here in the cottage while I go on assignments.'

Amber felt offended at what he was implying. With as much dignity as she could muster, she straightened and rose slowly, graceful in the long, rustling crushed-taffeta dress despite her Junoesque stature. With her flame-coloured hair floating around her flawless shoulders and her eyes blazing, she gave the impression of a woman on the warpath. Which she might be, if Jake pursued that line of thinking.

'Leo and I have been together since childhood. He's like a *brother* to me, nothing else! I don't understand why you're going on about it.'

'Because,' answered Jake tightly, 'people have been questioning what was going on between you two up here—'

'On my wedding day?' she broke in, shocked.

'You both seemed unusually wrapped up in each other,' he retorted. 'My journalist friends thought your behaviour was inappropriate. I have to say I agree with them.'

Amber went scarlet. She'd recognised the journalists, who'd been based in the African camp. They would have known about her passionate relationship with Enzo. Everybody did, because Enzo had made no secret of it. Presumably Leo's friends now thought that she made a habit of flinging herself at men.

'I see!' she muttered bitterly. Would her one mistake brand her for ever? 'I can't even hug a friend now! It's people's dirty minds, not my behaviour that you have to condemn!'

'I had to come up and take steps to scotch the rumours. I don't want any more gossip, Amber,' he said, his voice so softly laced with anger that it slid into her like a knife. 'We agreed that not only would you remain faithful to our marriage vows, but you'd be *seen* to be above suspicion. Keep to that agreement, Amber, or I'll wash my hands of you!'

She looked at him in dismay. The man she'd known—the caring man who'd brought her out of her nightmare and whom she'd witnessed carrying out so many acts of kindness—had vanished. Was this the real Jake? A suspicious, possessive man who expected her to be grateful to him because he'd given her baby the gift of legitimacy?

Desperately she clung to the memory of how he'd cheered up a group of women in a cellar in Sarajevo with an impromptu party. He'd played the piano, beautifully, meltingly, making them all cry. And then he'd danced with every one of them, while Amber had laughingly picked out one-finger tunes.

She made herself remember the time when he'd waded in, fists flying, to a group of men taking a sack of grain from a helpless woman. But that didn't help. It only reminded her that he had one hell of a temper when roused.

'What's happened to you?' she asked unhappily. 'We've got on so well together up to now. I thought we could be good friends!' Suddenly she realised just how important that promise of friendship had been to her. Without it, the marriage would be impossible. 'Jake,' she went on in a soft, shaky plea, 'don't change! Please don't start acting like a jealous lover—'

His head snapped up sharply, making the black curls dance. 'What the hell are you talking about?' he demanded. 'Of course I'm not jealous! But the last thing in the world I want is scurrilous gossip about my wife and Leo Brandon.'

His firm hand caught her chin and tipped her head up. A tongue of flame seemed to leap inside her. Sickness? No... Something different. Then what?

In case something in her eyes betrayed her confusion, she lowered her lashes resentfully. Jake's warm breath caused the remaining petals on her breast to lift and flutter over her pillowy curves.

And, alarmingly, a small ache centred itself in her loins as if her body briefly retained the memory of what it was like to be close to a man and desire him. Appalled, she repressed that feeling and leaned against the side of the gallery for support.

'I'm *not* promiscuous! You'll have no cause to worry about the future,' she said, her tone pleading with him to believe her. 'I behaved out of character with Enzo. I was emotionally vulnerable at the time. You know what it was like out there.'

'Heartbreaking,' he said flatly.

'Oh, yes!' Men had wept along with the women. 'In all the years I worked for Unite, that last assignment in Africa was the most painful. I've never known so many children to be separated from their parents. It drained me physically and emotionally. She bit her lip. 'Because my mother had died shortly before I went out, *I* was in need of comfort and affection too. But that's all in the past. I'm not likely to behave like that again.'

'Is that so? Perhaps it's in your nature to be emotionally impulsive. You're something of an enigma.' He studied her doubtfully. 'Sometimes you seem very innocent. Other times...'

She gulped at the sexual implication. And her skin crawled with fear as she felt herself respond to his powerful masculinity. 'Don't condemn me,' she husked.

'I don't. Nature is nature. You can't hide your needs. Most of the time you shut them away, but one day they'll surface. You're uninhibited—'

'I'm...*what*?'

'Forget it,' he said shortly. 'I'm sorry I mentioned it.'

A coldness settled around her heart. He'd heard something. 'Tell me what you mean!' she demanded hoarsely.

There was a long pause, then, 'All right. Perhaps then you'll understand my reservations about you,' he said grudgingly. 'At the camp you had quite a reputation: a demure woman with passionate depths. Enzo boasted about you—'

'Oh, no!' she groaned.

'I always walked away when he started talking about you. But once, when I was travelling in a van beside him, in convoy, with hostile gunmen all around, it was difficult to escape his reminiscences. I'm sorry,' he said shortly, seeing her distress. 'You did ask.'

Hidden from view in the shadowed corner of the gallery, she covered her face with her hands as her stomach rebelled and she fought valiantly to keep her dignity and *not* throw up. She was shaking like a leaf, appalled that everyone in the camp had been fed stories about the quality of her performance in bed.

'Oh-h-h! I feel awful! Go away! Leave me alone!' she muttered, feeling weak.

'I can't. We have a charade to play first.'

'A charade?' she echoed morosely.

'I hurried up here, leaving in mid-conversation,' he said grimly. 'They could all see why. I'd been glaring at you and Leo for several minutes, hoping you'd get the message. As far as anyone else is concerned, we've had a talk and you've explained that there's nothing between you and Leo. And you're going to show you're sorry to have worried me by flinging yourself into my arms and kissing me.'

She froze. Took one look at his sensual mouth and backed away to the shadowy rear of the gallery till her spine hit one of its supporting posts.

'We—we don't have to kiss.' She swallowed as an irrational fear clutched at her vocal cords. 'Why don't we just go down into the hall, walk about arm in arm and smile into each other's eyes?' she suggested hopefully.

His lifted eyebrow mocked her cowardice. 'It wouldn't be enough. It needs to be something passionate and definitive.'

'P-passionate?' She stumbled over the word.

'Come here where you can be seen. And make it look good,' he insisted sternly. 'It's important.'

Fighting the nausea, she tried to fix a smile on her face. 'Won't something like that do?'

His eyes flickered with annoyance. 'If you're not going to take this matter seriously...'

Her mouth drooped. 'Oh, it's serious. That's why I'm finding it so hard to look carefree. And besides, I hate deception!' she muttered rebelliously.

'So do I. But sometimes it's necessary,' Jake told her curtly. 'My body will shield you from view. They'll see what we're doing from the angle of my back.'

She hesitated.

'*Do it!*' he ordered.

Too weary, too sick to protest any longer, she stepped forward a pace or two.

'Wind your arms around my neck, Amber.'

She obeyed and laid her hands on the smooth nape of his neck. Springy black curls did their best to snake around her fingers and she concentrated on them as she stood on tiptoe and he wrapped his arms around her. Her eyes closed tightly.

His cool mouth met hers for what seemed like an eternity. And all she could feel was the nausea, pushing up from her stomach to her throat, threatening her dignity and her pride. So she moaned and tried to draw away, but Jake ruthlessly cupped the back of her head with his palm and drove her mouth deeper into his.

'Stay with it,' he muttered harshly against her lips. 'In my book, passion is supposed to last longer than twenty seconds.'

The kiss went on and on. She held herself tense and unresponsive, willing the nightmare to end. Dimly she became aware of Jake's hard mouth softening, coaxing her lips more sweetly. And for a dreadful, heart-stopping moment she felt herself responding. Terrified, she pushed at his hard chest and met a wall of steel, which budged not an inch.

It wasn't a pretend kiss-and-make-up kiss any longer. It had become something else. It was obvious that Jake's natural sexuality had begun to assert itself. She could feel the melting together of their bodies, the increase of his heartbeat against her crushed breast and the answering clamour of her own pulse.

His hands moved soothingly over her half-naked back and she gave an involuntary shudder of pleasure. Almost instantly, a new and predatory hunger overtook him and his mouth and body drove more confidently into hers.

A spasm of dark despair shot through her. She'd married Jake because he'd said that he'd never touch her. Because of her child, because of the black melancholy she'd felt after her affair and the deep, deep humiliation, she had wanted to stay in limbo, celibate for the rest of her life.

But the unthinkable had happened. Jake wasn't as indifferent as he had pretended.

Oh, God! she thought helplessly, petrified with horror. Jake had lied to her! He *did* intend passion to play a part in their relationship—and she was in danger of becoming aroused by him. That was the very last thing on earth that she wanted!

CHAPTER TWO

A BURST of applause sounded in Amber's ears—laughter too, and murmurs of approval. To her vast relief, Jake broke free, his expression unreadable.

'Success at last,' he said huskily. 'It took long enough to get a response, didn't it?' His eyes flickered to hers as if asking a question but she felt too confused to understand what that might be. He gave a wry smile. 'I thought no one would notice us for a while. I had visions of us locked mouth to mouth for another ten minutes at least.'

Then he turned and laughingly acknowledged their amused guests below as if nothing special had happened between them at all.

Her agitated breathing slowed, though she felt weak, as if he'd stolen all her energy. She licked her softened lips and gave a sigh of thanks. Aware of the tingling of her body, she knew that she had to escape to her room to recover her composure. Now that they'd 'made up' publicly, he couldn't object if she disappeared for a while.

'Jake,' she said, her voice still infuriatingly soft with arousal. She looked at him in alarm when he whirled around, smiling.

'It wasn't so bad, kissing me, was it?' His hand lightly touched her hair and she shrank back again into the dark recesses of the gallery, pressing against the rose garlands which hung in swags on the wall. 'Amber...I think you're in need of more comfort and affection than you realise,' he mused, his eyes drowsy and warm.

'No!' she managed to say. 'No, I'm not.'

'If you say so,' he murmured, a faint twinkle in his eyes.

How dared he twinkle, when panic was beginning to claw at her stomach? And she had no fight left in her to argue...

'Don't patronise me!' she complained feebly. 'I didn't want to be kissed. I didn't like it. I feel sick. I'm very tired too. That's why I didn't stop you when I wanted to.'

'I see,' he drawled lazily.

Amber passed a weary hand over her forehead. There had been too many emotional dramas, too many tears, too much for her to cope with. She'd never whined or whimpered before, but right now she felt like doing just that.

'I've had enough,' she said plaintively, her voice near to breaking. 'I'm at the end of my tether with everything that's happened to me recently. I'm falling apart—'

She stopped her muttered litany because Jake strode towards her and caught both of her shoulders in a firm grip. 'Shape up, Amber!' he advised sternly. 'If you're going to feel sorry for yourself then you'll never get through the next few hours.'

'Don't bully me! Go away!' she complained, dreading it all.

'I can't. We're married, remember?'

'But not welded together!'

'As good as, for the next hour,' he pointed out.

'No. I'm quitting now—'

'You can't,' he said patiently. 'Not yet. First I have to get something clear. And then you must give a convincing performance to all and sundry. I want there to be no doubt about your feelings for me.'

She gulped. No more kissing, though, no more touching, she thought. She didn't think she could bear it. 'That—that kiss was enough to convince people, surely? Jake, you can't ask me to do that again—'

'It depends on how well you act the loving bride,' he told her flatly. Amber gave him a puzzled look. He sounded...bitter. 'In a moment, you'll come down to the hall with me and you will sparkle like the diamonds on your finger. And dance with me as if you would die for me,' he added with mocking softness.

Feeling hot and giddy again, she tried to move to the chair but the back of her dress seemed to be caught somewhere at the waist. 'Oh, Jake—I'm trapped!' she cried in dismay, twisting to see where and how. And she wanted to cry tears of angry frustration. She could feel them filling her eyes, blurring her gaze as she stared miserably up at him.

He slipped his hand around her to investigate. 'So you are. Impaled on a rose thorn. Life's full of them, isn't it?'

There was a heady perfume in her nostrils, a waft of velvety scent as Jake's arm brushed against the thickly clustered briars. And something else that she was beginning to identify—sharper, warmer...the scent of Jake himself, the scent of man.

His cheek had moved unnervingly close to hers. Amber's big eyes slanted sideways. Jake's skin was like warm brown satin. At least, she presumed it was warm. Heat was coming off his body, filling the space between them.

Her heart seemed to be leaping all over the place but she had no idea why, only knew that he disturbed her and that she didn't feel safe any more.

'Jake! Set me free!' she demanded jerkily.

He gave a wry smile. 'That was my plan,' he murmured, both arms now firmly around her still slender waist. The lines of his mouth were butter-soft as his fingers fiddled at the small of her back. He looked at her obliquely, an amused glint in his eyes. 'Mind you, I don't think I can achieve that without some damage to—'

'My dress! Please be careful—'

'I think,' he said drily, 'the condition of your dress is the least of your problems.'

His meaning wasn't clear at first. And then it was. As he struggled to free her he shifted his weight so that his knee pressed into her skirt, crushing the petticoats against her thigh with a soft whisper of taffeta. A slight movement of his body brought his chest against her heart-shaped bodice again and she drew in a shuddering breath.

That wasn't deliberate, was it? Please not, she begged silently. She was imagining his interest. She had to be.

'Hurry up!' she muttered nervously.

'Don't fidget. You've got yourself into a right tangle and I'm the only person who can sort you out.' He smiled faintly as if he'd said something privately amusing. 'There! It's free— Stay still!' he ordered, when she made to knock away his arm. 'The veil's caught. Be patient.'

Her liquid brown eyes met his and flashed a hot defiance. 'Patient be blowed! I've had enough of this!'

Crossly she reached back, encountering his strong fingers. For a moment they both seemed to be wrestling with the stubborn sprays of roses and Amber became increasingly heated as she struggled to escape from Jake's unwelcome nearness.

'Nearly there,' he murmured casually.

'Oh, curse it!' she raged.

'Calm down, it's no big deal. Is it?' he breathed, in the region of her small, horribly sensitive ear.

Amber gritted her teeth and wrenched at the offending briar. Pain lanced through her hands. Warm blood trickled onto her palms. But she was free and the relief was overwhelming. Quickly she ducked and slipped sideways, beneath his encircling arm. And then to her dismay she felt his hand closing around her elbow, spinning her around.

'You fool!' he said gruffly.

And suddenly his warm mouth was pressing into her palm and his tongue was licking the small drops of blood there. Amber found that she couldn't move. Pale and frightened, she watched as if in a dream while he turned his attention to her other hand, nursing it, repeatedly catching each tiny drop of blood with his tongue.

A wave of despair swept through her. He'd only taken a few seconds over the gesture but his deeply tender and erotic action had made her unsure of his real motive for marrying her. She felt her knees buckle and his hand reached out to steady her.

'It's all right, Amber,' he soothed. 'Calm yourself. You can relax. Everything's fine. You've been scratched, you've bled a little, but there's no lasting damage. In a short time you'll hardly know you've been hurt.'

Hardly listening to what he was saying, more interested in *how* he was saying it, she snatched her hands from his, shaken by the resonating warmth of his husky drawl. As far as she was concerned, everything wasn't fine. Because in his dark eyes there had been an unmistakable flare of desire. In his mouth too, she thought in confusion as his lips parted over even white teeth.

Her head was spinning, the world whirling. The heat that flared in her body made her want to groan in despair. It was a sure sign that her nausea was returning. The prickling sensation swept relentlessly over her sensitive skin and she began to breathe faster. Much faster. Her lungs seemed empty in seconds.

'What is it?' he asked with a worrying tenderness.

'Let's get one thing straight,' she said, trying—and failing—to keep her voice even. 'I've been through hell. I feel terrible. Miserable. I—I—' Helpless tears filled her eyes and she groaned as her stomach rolled in a final warning. 'Oh, help!' she flung at him in panic, and rushed through the archway.

Picking up her skirts, she fled from Jake down the spiral steps, her hair and her veil flying out behind her like a banner. No sound came to her ears other than the harsh rasp of her own breathing and the tap of her satin slippers. Thank heavens, she thought, he'd decided not to follow her.

At last she reached the bottom of the tiny stairs and her feet were on the thickly carpeted landing. Ahead lay the sanctuary of the room which had been put aside for her that day. Getting there—alone—was all she could think of and she heaved open the heavy door with a moan of relief.

Safe at last. Slamming the door shut, she leaned her back against it, panting hard. And then she raced for the bathroom. A few minutes later she emerged, feeling pale and drained, her mass of flaming hair in disarray.

Only to find Jake, sprawled on the bed.

Her eyes widened till they were two huge dark smudges in her white face as he nonchalantly lifted his arms and made a cradle of them behind his head. Her throat dried. She felt too battered by life to cope with him.

'Not you!' she groaned rudely.

Amber watched him stretching like a contented cat. His arms were strong and sinewy, his lithe body displayed to full advantage on the oyster silk bedspread. He looked confident and dangerous, the line of his muscular thighs never more blatantly apparent than now, in the supremely masculine pose.

'Me,' he agreed implacably. 'We have to talk, Amber.'

'Talk?' she repeated weakly. That was the last thing she was expecting. The crippling weight of nausea and depression flowed through her. 'I can't face anything or anyone right now, Jake!' she muttered, hating herself for sounding so pathetic. But she knew that she was about to snap and wanted to be on her own when it happened. 'Give me ten minutes. I must be alone.'

'This can't wait,' he insisted. His eyes glittered beneath the thick fringe of black lashes. 'Bear with me, Amber. I need to know why you ran away from me just now and why you're so miserable. You seemed perfectly all right until you heard that Leo was leaving—and then you went to pieces. What am I to make of that?'

Amber strolled around the bed, hoping that she looked nonchalant, hoping that she could reach the door and make a graceful exit. And then, she thought, with a flash of her old humour, she'd be able to wail and gnash her teeth and shake as much as she wanted!

'It wasn't anything to do with him. If you must know, I ran off because I felt sick. I was scared of throwing up all over your DJ,' she answered, deciding to be blunt. That might curb any lurking passion! she thought waspishly.

Frowning, he slid his feet to the floor and stood up. 'When you came back to Castlestowe on the couple of occasions you were on leave from Africa... did you and Leo meet?' he asked quietly.

'Of course!'

'I presume your reunions were... affectionate? You were delighted to see him. You flung yourself into his arms.'

She shifted uncomfortably. 'Yes. Why not?' To her surprise, he winced. Hastily she sought to reassure him. 'I've told you, we're childhood friends. But I—I was going around with Enzo at the time, remember?' she reminded him, seeing where this was leading.

'Nevertheless, your emotions were in a turmoil,' he persisted soberly. 'When you came home each time, you felt exhausted and in need of a friend's loving warmth. You needed someone to soothe you, to help you forget the pain and suffering you'd left behind, because the mind can only take so much, can't it?'

'Yes! But—'

'If I recall, Leo was in need of love too.' Oddly, it sounded as though Jake was forcing himself to talk about her relationship with Leo. Judging by the pinched expression on his face, it wasn't something he relished. 'You told me,' he went on gruffly, 'that he and Ginny had been divorced and he was deeply unhappy.'

Her eyes darkened. 'You're implying I gave him sexual comfort!'

Amber gazed at him in open-mouthed astonishment. She was about to launch into a furious defence of herself when he sucked in a sharp breath and transfixed her with a lethal stare.

'What I have to know is this,' he growled, his voice shaking. 'Is there the remotest chance that your child might be Leo's?'

Shocked into silence for a moment, she struggled to find her voice. 'No!' she cried in horror. 'How dare you? He loves Ginny. He always has, always will—'

'You are *sure*?' he demanded, his muscles tense with anticipation. 'Absolutely, totally sure?'

'I swear on my mother's memory!' she said fervently.

Jake's raised shoulders relaxed and he let out all the air in his lungs as if he'd stored up doubts and uncertainties for a long and stressful time. The lines eased out of his face till he looked like the friendly Jake she knew and liked.

'Thank you,' he breathed. 'Forgive me if I've offended you, but I had to ask.'

'I'm puzzled,' she said slowly. 'Why don't you mind Enzo being the father of my child but dread the thought of it being Leo?'

He frowned and lowered his head. 'Enzo wouldn't jeopardise his marriage by putting in a claim to your child,' he said to his feet. 'Leo might have done if he'd been the father.'

'That matters?'

Slowly his head lifted till his veiled eyes met hers. 'I intend to commit myself to you and your child. I wouldn't want a legal battle for possession. I'm relieved it's Enzo who's the father.' His normally confident voice sounded shaky. 'Other than us, only your boss, Mary Smith of Unite, knows the truth. I want it to stay that way. No one must ever discover that I haven't fathered your child.'

She didn't reply immediately. Her eyes searched his face while she tried to work out why he should be so anxious. 'Why not?'

He hesitated. 'Pride,' he said after a while. 'I don't want to be seen as a cuckolded fool.'

Somehow she felt that that wasn't the right reason. It was so unlike him to put the opinion of others before what was right. 'A child should know its biological parents,' she said gently. 'Always. My child must be told about its father as soon as he or she can understand—'

'No!' he said emphatically, closing the space between them with rapid strides. 'Because of the unusual circumstances of our marriage, we have to give your child our love and a stable background. Maybe we'll never tell him or her the truth. Or we might decide it's appropriate in ten, twelve years or so—'

'Ten years?' She looked at him doubtfully. 'I don't know, Jake. It's such a big thing for me to decide now, when I'm muddled and unsettled.'

'Then I'll make it easier for you,' he said flatly. 'Agree that we postpone any decision to tell your child about Enzo for at *least* ten years and I will stay with you. Disagree and I leave you—now. So you can damn well think on your feet, Amber!'

She would have done, if her legs hadn't been giving up on her. It worried her that she might feel this feeble for the next month or so of her pregnancy.

His eyes burned into hers. Against her will she felt a sweep of helpless surrender. It had been like that when Jake had coaxed her into accepting his proposal. She'd been powerless then because her shock at Enzo's betrayal had left her limp and defenceless. For the first time in her life she hadn't cared what happened to her, and had been indifferent to the way that Jake had been taking over her life. He was doing so again.

'I suppose,' she said, struggling to think rationally, 'you're right about making my child feel secure first but—'

'No buts. Promise,' he insisted. 'OK. You asked for this. I didn't want to spell it out, but you have to think of the consequences, Amber! Your child would need to be older than you think to cope with the news that you had an adulterous affair.'

'Jake!' she protested.

His eyes flickered at her involuntary gasp of anguish. And suddenly his tone gentled to a soft huskiness which carried a wealth of heart-warming tenderness in it. 'I'm trying to get you to see what it would feel like, both for you and your child.' He paused, his eyes full of compassion. 'Imagine that you yourself discovered that, oh, for instance *neither* of your parents have any blood ties to you.'

'Awful!' she acknowledged fervently.

'Worse, you heard that your biological father was a liar, a cheat and an adulterer who didn't think twice about breaking his marriage vows.'

She gave a little shudder of distaste, dreading the moment when her child learnt about its father. 'I take your point. If that happened to me, I'd go to pieces!'

His eyes flickered with pity. 'Yes. You might...unless you had a lot of support to cope with the revelation. You'd feel hurt and bewildered.' He adopted a casual tone, but she couldn't help noticing that he kept fiddling with his cuffs. That wasn't like him. Just as she was about to probe his feelings he said with a rather unnatural lightness, 'And you'd feel shame? Hatred, maybe?'

'I think I would,' she admitted.

Jake seemed inordinately relieved. 'And so would your innocent child. This is why many fostered or adopted children aren't told of their background,' he said gently.

'Perhaps,' she agreed, surprised at his perception. And she thought of the future—telling her child about Enzo and trying to explain how she'd been stupidly infatuated with a philanderer. It was a horrible image. Jake was right; her child would surely turn from her.

'Then we're agreed. Your baby must be accepted as my own, without question,' he said with an easy smoothness, as if he'd rehearsed those very words.

But by marrying her and taking on her child as his own Jake would have an heir without Cavendish blood. And that wasn't what he wanted, surely? She struggled to understand and wished that she felt more alert. The answer was all bound up in her child somehow, but she couldn't for the life of her work it out.

'You weren't exactly on the shelf,' she declared. 'Given time, you could have found someone you loved.'

'In my job?' He lifted his shoulders in a dismissive shrug. 'I'm always on the move. It doesn't give any relationship a fighting chance. And of the dozens of women I have met I've loved none. I can't let go, you see. And women want me to. They like emotional commitment. I don't have it in me. And don't ask me about my past,' he said, when she opened her mouth to do just that.

There was a wounded look to his eyes which stopped her from pursuing the mystery. Instead she remained silent, keeping to herself the knowledge that something traumatic in his background had made him determined to protect his emotions.

She remembered his reaction whenever she'd touched on her happy home life and wondered if his parents had been repressive or cold. But he'd spoken of them with love earlier. And Mrs Cavendish had sounded warm and affectionate on the telephone.

It was as she'd thought; it must have been a romance that had gone sour. Surprisingly, that disturbed her.

'What about it, Amber?' he asked persuasively. 'I'd prefer not to disillusion my parents about their grandchild at this time—or about you.' She winced. His parents would be appalled if they knew the truth. 'Nor,' he continued with a winning smile, 'do we want any family member pronouncing our son or daughter illegitimate and claiming the Cavendish fortune when I die, do we?'

'Or the Fraser fortune!' she said wryly.

Jake flashed her a suspicious look then relaxed when he saw that she was mocking her own lack of funds. 'That's settled,' he said decisively. 'As far as everyone's concerned, your child is mine. It's for the best, Amber. Enzo won't care, will he?'

She winced again, shame flooding her face with colour as she remembered the humiliating rejection scene. 'He washed his hands of his responsibilities.'

Jake nodded sympathetically. 'It's over. Life will begin again for you.'

But Amber felt like crying. The future seemed bleak without the prospect of a man she could love in her life. Desperate to stay calm, she turned away, walked over to the window and stared into the darkness. 'I wish I could believe that.'

'You can't shut yourself off for ever,' he murmured softly.

Hearing the coaxing message in his tone, she whirled around, half-blind with the film of tears. 'You don't understand how badly I feel about myself! I mean to keep my head below the parapet in future! I'll *never* forget what it's been like to feel disgusted with myself for abandoning my self-respect.'

Jake made a consoling gesture. 'You were the victim of an expert seducer—'

'I succumbed. He didn't force me,' she admitted honestly. 'It's been a nightmare, Jake—one I've deserved. I blame myself for being stupid.' She felt herself drooping with exhaustion. 'Don't expect anything of me, other than the friendship I'm sure we can share. I'll be a good wife and a good mother and a good companion. Please don't ask any more of me—I can't give it. Mary Smith thinks the world of you and I respect her judgement. I'm trusting you to leave me alone. In return, I'll agree to keep my child's origin a secret for the time you suggest. You have my word.'

'Thank you,' he said quietly. 'And I'll do my best to be a good father whenever I'm around. I know that you'll more than compensate for my absences. You have a natural way with children, Amber. The refugee kids loved you. And you gave them a great deal: laughter, comfort, love...'

His voice was husky but unthreatening and she warmed to Jake, the man she admired, who'd spoken gently to her when she was so hurt and who'd made her begin her life again. He'd given her a way out of her hell, some hope, some dignity.

Her spirits rose a little. The future would be better than the past, she told herself. It had to be. She had no reserves of strength to cope with any more distress.

'The children had lost everything,' she said pensively. 'And I've had such a loving family. I know how awful I felt when each of my parents died. A gap opened in my life that'll never be filled. Stuart did his best, but it wasn't the same as having my father around. Dad was part of me, you see—my flesh and blood.'

'And you adored your mother, you said.' Jake sounded as if he understood her emptiness.

'I miss her dreadfully,' she admitted. 'That's why I could empathise with the displaced children. That's why I worked so hard to find their parents for them. My parents were everything to me. Loyal, truthful, totally straight—'

'Yes, yes...' Jake wouldn't look at her. He shifted uncomfortably, as if her confidences embarrassed him. 'Don't build up your parents to be gods in your mind, Amber,' he said in warning. 'Don't put them on a pedestal. It's a mistake—'

'Not in their case.' Her eyes shone softly. 'They were special and I'm proud to be their daughter.'

'No one is perfect,' he persisted, much to her annoyance. 'Even they might have had failings or secrets they'd have preferred kept hidden.'

'I won't hear a word against them!' she declared indignantly, a little uneasy with the solemn, almost pitying way he was looking at her. Tiredness swept over her and she sighed. 'I feel drained.'

'Poor Amber. You're shaking like a leaf. It's all become too much for you to handle, hasn't it? Why don't you lie down for a while?'

The bed looked welcoming. But, strangely, so did he. Her urge to throw herself into his arms was rather unnerving. 'I think I'd better keep going,' she said thinly. 'I'll spend a little time with our guests and then perhaps we can leave.' She took a few unwilling steps towards the door.

'Wait a minute. You can't go like that,' Jake said in a kindly tone. 'Your veil is crooked and you look very wan with no make-up on your face.'

'Oh!' Amber heaved a sigh. 'I am a bit of a mess. I forgot. Thanks.'

'You're not a mess. You're very beautiful. Rather fragile and ethereal,' he said quietly.

She blinked in surprise, at a loss for an answer. Nervously she picked up her skirts, rustling her way to the dressing table, and sat down to make the adjustments. Her hands were stiff and awkward and she couldn't make them do what she wanted them to.

While she fumbled in her make-up bag for a lipstick, her attention kept straying to Jake, who was reflected in the mirror. The warm slide of his encouraging smile made her drop the lipstick on the floor. She bent down for it and knew the minute it was in her shaking hands that she'd never be able to use it. She'd end up looking like a clown.

'Try the powder,' he suggested.

'I was going to.' Hastily she dabbed at her face with a sable brush. 'Look, I'm edgy. Do you have to watch?' she muttered, uncomfortable with his intense scrutiny.

'I think I ought to stay with you,' he replied.

His voice had deepened to a husky growl that reached all the way down to her wriggling toes and all the way up again, doing odd things to her body on the way.

She slammed the powder-compact down. 'It's no good! I can't face the guests,' she said in dismay, dreading the thought of having to pretend to flirt with Jake.

'Yes, you can,' he said firmly. 'Like some help with your lipstick?' he offered.

She froze. He took two strides towards her. She felt her heart soar to the roof of her mouth, and before she could drag it back down again he'd dropped to his haunches in front of her, picked up the lip pencil she'd been agitatedly fiddling with and was holding her chin firmly between his finger and thumb.

'I'm quite good at this,' he said reassuringly.

'Not as good as me!' she squeaked.

He smiled in amused disagreement. 'Have you seen your hands? Hold still.'

The velvety whisper kept her paralysed in the chair. Jake slowly brought the pencil towards her mouth. Amber held her breath and watched the lazy flutter of his incredibly long eyelashes as they lowered almost to the sword-blade cheekbones. His concentration was spellbinding and she was its prisoner, captured by the sensual beauty of his face.

Quite irrationally afraid, she let the pencil softly shape the full curves of her mouth. It felt deeply erotic, having Jake do that for her, but she couldn't move, couldn't breathe, didn't dare to speak. Because she knew that she'd croak like a frog and he'd misinterpret her confusion.

'Open,' he coaxed, smiling charmingly.

Her lips had parted for him before she could stop them. She closed her eyes to shut out his handsome face. It was too sexy, too dangerous and too near. The faint drift of his breath lifted all the tiny hairs around her mouth. Next she felt the stroke of the creamy lipstick around the high arch of her mouth and then it was gliding over her full lower lip very, very slowly. Too slowly.

And then it stopped. Jake's breathing rasped louder. Somehow she forced her eyes open. He was looking at her as though transfixed.

So quickly did he jump to his feet that she jerked her head around to check her reflection in the mirror and see what had startled him. Two hot spots of colour burned on her cheeks. Her mouth seemed to be pouting an indolent invitation. She peered closer. Was that because of the way he'd painted it? Or had her apparent allure startled him?

'Here.' Apparently quite detached, Jake passed her a tissue to blot her lips. 'Anything else you want me to adjust?' he asked lightly. 'Corsets, false leg, suspenders?'

'I can manage!' she said, hastily fixing her hair, lifting her arms in a graceful arc.

'Ready for our dance, then?' he murmured.

Somehow she managed to smile, her lips a bright splash of colour in her white face. But she gazed in growing consternation at his compelling face with its wickedly expressive mouth and come-to-bed eyes. No, she couldn't dance with him, let alone look as if she'd die for him. Nor did she want to go back to the cottage with him. Caught between a rock and a hard place...

To her dismay she began to cry.

'Oh, darn it!' she mumbled furiously.

'You're in an emotional mess, aren't you? I thought this might happen,' Jake said sympathetically. He lifted her hand from where it clutched the dressing table and watched it trembling limply, dwarfed by his large palm. She hoped that he hadn't seen how white her knuckles were. 'You're exhausted,' he said with a frown. 'I think

you ought to call it a day. You've got a lot ahead of you
yet.'

Amber scowled at the ominous prediction. 'You'd be
exhausted,' she said sulkily, 'if you'd been fighting off
nausea for the last few hours.'

Abandoning her hand, he came to stand behind her
and lightly rested his fingers on her tense shoulders.
Amber gritted her teeth because she wanted to risk
throwing her arms around him. Their eyes met in the
mirror and she watched his frown deepen.

'You're right on the edge, aren't you?' Although he
didn't take his eyes off her scared face, his fingers increased their pressure, searching the tight muscles with
a blissfully deep massage. 'The whole of your body is
screwed into knots.'

'OK, so it is! Is it surprising? I've thrown my lot in
with you and I'm not sure—' She gasped as his fingers
paused and bit into her flesh.

'There's no going back,' he said evenly. 'We agreed.
We're bound together for the rest of our lives.'

Wearily she lifted her head, desperate to get away from
Jake's maddeningly relaxing caresses. 'Help me get
through this!' she whispered.

'A few minutes downstairs,' he promised, 'and then
I'll insist that we leave.'

'I—I want to be totally alone tonight, Jake,' she said,
staying his hand when he made to help her up. 'Could
you sleep somewhere else—and collect me in the
morning?'

'I'm sorry,' he said shortly, 'it's out of the question.'
He hesitated as if he was choosing his words and then
said decisively, 'You see, Amber, I have something to
tell you when we reach your cottage—something I think
you ought to know about your parents.'

CHAPTER THREE

IT FELT like an eternity before Amber and Jake were walking along the moonlit path to her cottage with the celebratory skirl of bagpipes receding into the background. On an impulse, she turned and waved to Stuart, who stood alone and was easily identifiable because he was as big as a barn door and had hair as untamable and as red as hers. Yet his appearance made her more anxious than ever. His huge, kilted figure seemed uncharacteristically hunched and anxious.

'Bye, darling!' she cried, but her light voice was caught by the breeze and probably never reached her godfather. And anyway, there was a lump in her throat which prevented her from shouting more loudly.

'Ring me at Westminster if you need me!' he roared, and she heard the guests chuckling.

Despite her worries, she smiled too. Dear Stuart! His bellow was capable of reaching the Highland cattle grazing half a mile away! And it was absurd that a young bride would need a gruff old bear like Stuart, unless...unless he knew that there was trouble ahead, of course.

An icy shiver ran through her body and Jake shed his jacket instantly. 'Here,' he said, watching her carefully as he placed it around her shoulders.

'Thanks.' The satin lining was warm and sensuous. It smelled of him, and his courteous gesture comforted her a little.

Knowing that people were watching from the terrace, she let him curve an arm around her waist. But it meant that he could feel how much she trembled.

Her nerves had been in shreds when Jake had insisted that he wouldn't tell her anything till they were alone in her cottage. Then he'd led her down to the great hall. It had been nearly two in the morning yet everyone had still seemed full of steam and had seemed to be having a wonderful time.

Newly alert, she'd become aware of Stuart's anxious brown eyes frequently resting on her. And also that an unmistakable hostility had sprung up between Jake and Stuart. Previously, in the days leading up to the wedding, they'd got on well together, but something had changed since then. She'd sensed a grim determination on Jake's part and a reproach—almost a pleading—on Stuart's.

Pleading? Tough, gruff, silent-in-adversity Stuart? Amber had felt more alarmed than ever. Their mutual antagonism had probably something to do with what Jake knew about her parents. Obviously Stuart didn't want her to be told. And a fear of the unknown had gnawed away at her mind till she'd felt like screaming.

Jake had taken control, calling for a slow waltz and sweeping her onto the dance floor. She'd buried her head in his shoulder because she hadn't been able to keep a smile on her face, no matter how hard she'd tried. People had probably thought that it was romantic. If only they knew!

The soft music, the candlelit hall, the dazzling ball-gowns and vibrant tartans had made no impression on her at all. Her mind had been preoccupied with wondering what her parents could have done—and how Jake knew about it.

They'd lived their whole lives on the Castlestowe estate, a few miles south of Oban, on the west coast of

Scotland. Her father, Angus, had been the laird's gillie and deermaster. Elizabeth Fraser had been a devoted wife and mother.

Her love-filled memories of her parents and her deep affection for Castlestowe were the only constant strengths in her life. Nothing must shake those foundations, she thought fervently. She was at a low emotional ebb at the moment and she needed to cling to something good and solid.

Her father had died twelve years ago and Stuart had let her mother stay in the tied cottage while she, Amber, continued to be privately educated at Stuart's expense. It had been a generous gesture to his favourite god-daughter.

Now the cool May air chilled the warmth of her face as they walked away from the party, but it was fresh, pure air—the champagne breath of western Scotland. She inhaled it, filling her lungs, gathering courage.

And then she pulled away from Jake and walked alone for a little way before she said in a strangled voice, 'My parents, Jake. Tell me before I go crazy!'

'I will. Wait till we get to your cottage,' he said.

She wanted to punch him, to turn and pummel that chest, heavy with muscle, till she got some kind of re-action other than the smug 'I know what's best for you' tone he'd adopted.

'This is my life you're toying with,' she said jerkily, trying to control her angry frustration. 'My parents and Stuart and Castlestowe mean everything to me—'

'I know. I'm not blind,' he said edgily.

His tone put her horribly on edge too. He sounded like a man who was about to tell a child that there was no Santa Claus.

Amber glanced at Jake, watching the wind whip the black curls into disarray. There was a stillness about him, an air of tense anticipation, and she felt her heart beat faster and faster with every step she took. Judging by the set of his face, he wasn't going to be swayed.

Seething, she bit back her anger. At least she could make sure that there was one constant area in her life. She'd push the virtues of Castlestowe for all she was worth.

'Then you'll understand that I want you to love it here as much as I do. So much has happened to me ... I need to stay here. I need the security of my home,' she said with shaky fervour, gesturing with her hand to the distant moors.

'You left willingly enough to work for Unite,' he pointed out casually.

'I did,' she admitted. 'I had an offer out of the blue, when I was in my last term at university. Mary Smith came to give a talk to our group. We got chatting and she offered me a job on the spot. I couldn't turn it down; it was such a wonderful opportunity.'

Far in the distance she could just discern the white sand beach and the waves crashing on the rocks, their thunder a sweet, familiar music in her ears. And some way ahead further still were the moors where her cottage nestled with its softly welcoming light glowing in the porch.

'When I was away I missed Castlestowe,' she continued. 'That's why I worked myself into the ground.' He knew how deeply she felt, she thought in relief when he nodded. 'I was very homesick. But I knew the refugee children would be homesick too, and they were so little, Jake! However sad I felt at being away from home, I knew I could never live with myself if I ran back and left them to their fates.'

'Quite a sacrifice,' he observed with an open admiration which made her feel better about herself.

'All children should be with their parents, Jake. I feel very strongly about that.'

In a quick movement he turned from her and scanned the horizon—but not before she'd registered a harshness deepening the lines of his face. Perhaps he missed his parents and was worried about his father, she thought sympathetically.

'I imagine it can be wild up here in the winter,' he said, as if making polite conversation.

Amber accepted his avoidance of a painful subject. At least she had an opportunity to expand on her love for her homeland. And it passed the time. They had a way to go before they reached the cottage.

'Ferocious,' she said with a half-laugh. 'The gales blow us off our feet, rain falls like stair-rods, and when it snows the blizzards heap up in great drifts that trap us indoors for days.'

'And you like that?' he asked wryly.

A gentle smile lit her face. 'It's exciting. Invigorating. Bad weather draws us all together. There's a comradeship I've never found anywhere else. We're one big family. People don't move house as they do elsewhere. Everyone's been here for generations and a kind of mutual caring knits the community together. When my mother died last year Stuart took care of me. Leo did too—and everyone else here.' Her huge eyes met Jake's. 'It's the love of old friends. The only kind of love I trust.'

His arm came around her shoulders. A steadying arm, as if she might need support. Amber was too apprehensive to shrug it off this time. 'There are other beautiful places in the world,' he suggested casually. 'Wilder, gentler, more remote...'

'Not for me!' she declared passionately. 'Where else is there a loch as beautiful as this—' she gestured '—with a surface like black glass and views to the Isle of Mull? Or where I can lie in the purple heather and watch the sun glittering on the sea and be swamped in total silence?'

He stopped and she stood there, her bridal gown shimmering in the moonlight, her hair tumbling down her back and her pale face dominated by her impassioned dark eyes. Slowly he took her in his arms with such a look of tenderness that she felt as though she was falling into the silky black loch. Afraid of what was happening to her, she would have run if she could, but her legs were made of lead.

'It was very brave of you,' he said thoughtfully, 'to put aside your feelings and leave your home again so soon after your mother's death. I have to say, however, that I think it was unwise of you to rush off to Africa. Why didn't you give yourself time to grieve?'

He raised a questing finger and she watched, hypnotised, as he lifted a wanton strand of her hair from where it had blown onto her mouth. With an effort, she pulled herself together.

'Stuart thought I needed to bury myself in work,' she husked. 'My instincts told me I wasn't ready, but he was so insistent...'

'Was he.' It was a statement, as if he'd known and deplored the influence of her godfather.

'I was aware there was so much to be done,' she explained, springing to Stuart's defence. 'Every day the television news was showing the most tragic pictures in Africa. I couldn't put myself first. I locked up my mother's things without looking at them and went.'

It had, however, been a mistake as far as she was concerned. Her emotions hadn't stood up to the enormous pressures—which had driven her into Enzo's arms. It was something she'd regret for the rest of her life.

'I'm sorry you've had such a hard time,' Jake said gently.

Imperceptibly she swayed closer towards him and hastily corrected the movement. She could easily find herself turning to him for comfort, she thought wanly. That would be a mistake too.

'Jake... I'm bone-weary. I want to get home and curl up. I want to shut the world out and everyone in it,' she confessed.

'Hold on,' he encouraged. 'Hold on.'

If only she could! It was taking all her will-power not to fling her arms around his waist and lay her head on his shoulder. To ask him to hold her, stroke her hair, murmur soothing things to her. She needed comfort. More than anything. It would be so easy to surrender. A small gesture, a sigh, to release the need for affection that she was carefully hiding from him...

With a great effort, she fought her desire to relax because she worried where that might lead. But she felt a weakness stealing over her, and with it a warm glow as her eyes closed drowsily and her treacherous body grew languid with what she thought must be exhaustion.

'I can't hold on!' she mumbled wearily. 'I feel as if I've reached rock-bottom, Jake.'

'Hell!' he muttered, tightening his grip on her waist. He seemed to hesitate and then, to her astonishment, he jerked her sharply so that her drooping head flipped up in a sudden movement and her misty eyes were being sizzled by his fierce gaze. 'I thought you had backbone!' he accused her. 'You never gave up so easily in the camps.'

'I couldn't give way,' she replied wearily. 'Not in public, anyway.'

'You toughed it out, I know. But you cried in Mary's arms sometimes,' he said bluntly.

'Mary told you that?' she asked, shocked. 'But . . . she *never* gossips!'

'She does to me.'

'Oh.' Amber felt faintly betrayed. Mary had become more than a friend to her. She'd confided all her hopes and fears for the future to Mary and had entrusted the older woman with her innermost thoughts. It was a shock to find that Jake was on equally close terms with her mentor.

'And you're starting to fall apart again. You can't do that now,' he stated flatly.

'Why not?' she muttered resentfully.

He angled his dark head and studied her for a while. And just as she began to find her breath shortening and becoming erratic with an irrational apprehension he said inexplicably, 'Because you need to be ready for a fight.'

Her stomach contracted. 'What do you mean?' she breathed.

Jake took a long time to answer and then he dropped a bombshell with breathtaking casualness. 'I was wondering how you'd react if I said that I don't ever want us to live here. Suppose I don't like this windswept, barren corner of Scotland and demand that we go elsewhere? What then?'

It was unthinkable. There was a roaring in her ears and her eyes widened in horror at his cruel taunts. 'Barren? It's not barren!'

'Have you ever been to a tropical jungle, Amber?' he asked mildly. 'Where bananas and frangipani and mangoes grow like weeds, where there are flowers all year long—'

'And there are no seasons,' she retaliated, the moonlight catching the flint in her eyes. 'No blanket of snow on the hills, no mists hanging in the glen, no sun making the scales iridescent on the back of a salmon when it leaps—'

'You think it's paradise here—'

'Yes! I do!' she cried, her heart sinking at his derogatory tone. He hated Castlestowe—and wanted her to leave! 'I—I'd banked on you not caring where you lived! Jake! I'd have to stay... I couldn't go, not now; it would break my *heart*!'

'I thought it was broken already,' he pointed out calmly, ignoring the flash of fury which tautened her mouth. 'And since you seem to have no guts at the moment,' he said, almost as if deliberately goading her, 'I feel confident that I could persuade you to leave if I so wished.'

'Like hell you could!' she ground out through her teeth. A great rush of strength came from nowhere, straightening her spine and putting the fight back into her heart. Guts? She'd give him guts! 'Maybe a while ago you might have pushed me in whatever direction you wanted. I accepted that in Africa I virtually became a zombie when Enzo abandoned me. You took over my life, making arrangements, decisions... All I wanted was to get home and whatever else happened to me seemed unimportant. But this is different,' she added with vigour. 'Now you're threatening everything I hold dear!'

'A small cottage in remote Scotland?' he queried, raising a disparaging eyebrow.

'It means more to me than anywhere else on earth!' she fumed. 'I will never leave! Never! I'd divorce you first! Do you hear that?'

'I hear.' He seemed amused. Or was that pleasure flitting across his mouth and eyes? 'Half of Scotland must be hearing too.'

'I don't care! Let them!' Wild with temper, she flung her hair back in a gesture of grim defiance. 'This is unpardonable, Jake! You waited till we were married to say this, hoping I'd be so damn grateful to you for saving my reputation that I'd trail around behind you like a meek child, docile and tractable, providing a convenient heir for the Cavendish family without any effort on your part and obeying your every command because life had reduced me to a miserable, mindless cabbage—'

'For a woman who felt faint and had reached rock-bottom you're remarkably energised! And so angry!' he marvelled with infuriating good humour.

'You don't know how angry!' she flared. 'The words "explosive" and "murderous" spring to mind!' He smiled, enraging her further.

'Oh, spare me the enigmatic smirk!' she snapped. 'You ought to be ashamed of the way you've treated me. You offered me a marriage of convenience—convenient for what?' she hurled at him. 'Your lust? Tired of chasing women about the world, are you?' she taunted. 'You pretended to be indifferent to me, but you're not, are you? Do you want someone conveniently waiting for you to be at your beck and call when you get back home? And where is that home to be? Where would you like me? Paris? Timbuktu? Tell me and I'll run there. I'll lie down like a doormat and you can walk all over me!' she finished sarcastically, reaching boiling point.

There was a horrible silence while Jake eyed her with a detached interest. And a mystifying satisfaction. 'At last,' he said in evident relief. 'The flame ignites.'

'Flame?' she spat.

'Flame,' he said, apparently highly pleased with himself. 'It was about time.'

'You've landed up with more than flames! You've put a match to a volcano!' she said hotly. 'How dare you play your sophisticated mind games with me? I took you on trust—and when you said we'd be friends and we'd have a mutual partnership it never occurred to me that I ought to get your words checked over by a *lawyer* in case you started to act like a slippery, double-crossing cheat!'

'Tough when you're threatened, aren't you?' he mused, infuriatingly unaffected by her tirade. 'I'm relieved. I did wonder what you were made of for a minute.'

'Tough? Me?' She flipped her red hair forward with a flick of her head. 'Look at that colour!' she snapped. 'It's my link with the Celts and I'm proud of it! You want to know how tough I am? Push me much further and you'll find out,' she grated. Her eyes gleamed with the light of battle. 'Try to force me to do anything against my will and I'll show you claws and teeth you'll never forget!'

He gave a faint smile. 'I wouldn't dream of forcing you. You're halfway where you need to be already.' Suddenly the amusement was wiped from his face. 'I'm preparing you. Nothing more sinister,' he added ominously.

'Preparing me for what?' she flashed.

'Surprises.' They didn't sound nice from the way he said that.

'Such as?' she demanded warily.

'Where we're going to spend our honeymoon after our night in the cottage.'

'We? You're probably going on your own!' she retorted sourly.

'You'll come,' he said with a quiet confidence.

Annoyed at his arrogance, she tipped up her chin belligerently and fixed him with her blazing eyes. 'Oh, will I? What paradise have you organised for this honeymoon?' she asked scathingly.

'The Caribbean. I booked us into a hide-away retreat in St Lucia.'

Amber stared at him in blank astonishment. 'But...that's where Ginny is! Leo will be there by to-night—'

'I know!' exclaimed Jake with manufactured amazement. 'Isn't it an extraordinary coincidence?'

'Extraordinary,' she said suspiciously. 'Did you tell Leo where you'd booked?'

'No. I gather,' he added in a conversational tone, 'that Ginny appears to have traced her father.'

She shot him a puzzled glance. 'McKenzie? I didn't know she'd lost touch with him.'

'No, I mean her real father. Ginny was adopted. The McKenzies aren't her natural parents.'

'I didn't know that!' exclaimed Amber in surprise.

'Her father is a plantation owner in St Lucia—a man called Vincente St Honoré.' Jake spoke as if the name was significant—someone famous, perhaps. But she'd never heard of the man.

'Leo said nothing about this!' she said, a little resentfully.

'I imagine he didn't want to go into lengthy explanations when he had a plane to catch. I'm told the old man is dying.' Jake lifted his dark head and stared sightlessly into the distance, as if he was seeing something else, somewhere else. 'Poor guy,' he said, not sounding sorry at all. 'It would seem that St Honoré has no one to love him because he's alienated everyone he's ever known.'

Amber's eyes narrowed. 'You seem remarkably well informed. Did Leo tell you all this?'

'Stuart, actually.'

She flushed. 'He could have let me know. I'm more family than you.'

'Yes,' mused Jake with a strange half-smile tipping the corners of his mouth, 'you are. But Stuart knew I'd

pass on the news. Convenient, isn't it, having Leo and
Ginny on the same island as us? If my company bores
you, you'll be able to spend some time with them. In
any case it'll be interesting to see this plantation that
Ginny expects to inherit.'

'I don't want to go to St Lucia,' Amber told him flatly.
'I'm staying here. You think you can threaten to take
me away from Castlestowe—but I won't move! Even if
it means our marriage folds.' Her breath caught in her
throat as an image came to her of Jake waving a final
goodbye and striding out of her life. Angry tears filled
her eyes. Why was he being so difficult? 'You're deliberately trying to break us up! I know it!' she cried
heatedly. 'You hate the prospect of living here. You regret
marrying me—'

'No!' he said testily. 'You're wrong! I'm trying to jerk
you into life! I'm trying any means I can to get some
kind of response from you—anything to yank you out
of your self-obsession.'

She glared. 'You worm!'

Jake seemed unaffected by her anger. 'I had to find
something that you cared about and threaten it,' he said,
as if he'd acted perfectly reasonably.

'Castlestowe?' she demanded. 'Those threats about
living somewhere else were a *ruse*?'

'Desperate measures,' he explained, not the faintest
hint of penitence in his voice. 'You've been drifting about
like a wet weekend, feeling sorry for yourself, ever since
you found out about Enzo—'

'I was hurt, you brute!' she snapped, appalled that
he should be so insensitive.

'I *know*!' He pushed an exasperated hand through his
hair. 'Amber, surely you can't forget how I cared for
you at that time?'

'No, I haven't forgotten,' she said sullenly. 'But that makes it all the harder to understand why now—'

'Now you're apathetic and listless. And you can't be, not at this time. You have to get a grip on yourself. You've got a lot of difficult adjustments to make.'

'They'll only be difficult if you keep on bullying me!' she flung at him furiously.

Jake nodded. 'Better,' he said approvingly. 'You're not as self-pitying as you were earlier.'

'Self...!' she spluttered.

'Yes! And you know it. The trouble is that you've always had a strong male figure in your life, and when you didn't have one around you searched and found Enzo. When he failed to live up to your expectations, you decided to run home and hide. You wanted to let everyone else take over for you. Stuart, Mary, me...'

'So? Everyone wants to crawl under a blanket and hide sometimes,' she muttered sulkily, digesting his accusation. *Had* she always leaned on others?

'But this isn't the time to go to ground,' he replied sharply. 'You'll need all the grit you can find. And now that I've stirred you up and got you fighting again—'

'You are so arrogant!' she cried, seething at the underhand way he'd roused her temper. 'You're not a puppeteer and I'm not Pinocchio! I won't have you playing God with my emotions.'

'I'm not,' he said grimly. 'Life is. It's going to fling you a few curves, Amber.'

'Why? There's only one person around here who would dream of harming me and it's you!' she cried heatedly.

His grip tightened like a steel band. 'No. I wouldn't harm you. I need you too much.'

Stopped in her tracks, she gulped, her body tense with nerves. 'Need?' Somehow she flung him a defiant look.

'What—what exactly do you need me *for*?' she asked jerkily.

His gaze was guarded as it shifted from her blazing eyes to her tightly clenched teeth and back to her eyes again. 'To need *me*.'

'Like hell I will!' she said defiantly, going deathly pale. Her mouth felt as if it was filled with ashes. Her stomach too. Rebelliously she glared at him, her hopes for an uncomplicated future dashed.

'You will need me,' he insisted quietly. 'Sooner than you know.'

He was very serious. Amber went cold, the sense of dread lurching back to grip her stomach with icy claws. 'What is this secret that concerns my parents?' she asked in a low whisper.

He seemed preoccupied with the red waterfall of her hair, his hand pushing it back from her gleaming shoulders. The touch of his fingers there and then on the nape of her neck made her draw in her breath involuntarily.

'Something that will test your courage,' he said softly.

She gasped and let out a strangled cry. 'Jake...'

His eyes lingered on the curve of her jaw...the bow of her lush mouth. His words sank into Amber's stunned brain. Every muscle in her body was tensed to straining point as he shot her a sharp, appraising glance.

'I think we'd better get back to the cottage while you're still on fire, hadn't we?' he said wryly. 'I'm sure we could both do with a dram of whisky to stiffen the sinews.'

Without waiting for her answer, he took her elbow in one hand and slipped his arm around her waist so firmly that she had no option but to hurry along beside him. The relentless pace gave her no chance to think why her sinews might need stiffening—and maybe it was just as well.

The prospect of what lay ahead both repelled and drew her. But she needed to know the secret which concerned her parents.

When they reached the door of her small cottage, he hesitated and gave her a long thoughtful look. 'Shall I carry you over the threshold?'

Instinct made her want to say yes. To be swept up in his arms and held close would be comforting. But he'd only scorn her for being weak. With difficulty she denied herself.

'No. It isn't a proper marriage.' Suddenly she felt overwhelmingly sad. 'There's no reason for us to indulge in romantic gestures,' she muttered, and sensed that he'd drawn away from her.

'Whatever you like.'

'Silence would be nice!' she retorted with a waspish snap.

With an expression as hard and ungiving as carved granite, he opened the door for her and they stepped inside. The tension stretched between them like overstrained harp strings. Wanting to scream, *Tell me!* at him, Amber controlled the urge and went to light the hurricane lamp with a taper. To her exasperation, her hand was shaking too much. Jake appeared at her side and steadied her trembling fingers, guiding them to the wick. It seemed to take an uncomfortably long time.

For some reason she'd stopped breathing. In the end her lungs finally protested, and she gulped in air, and she quickly moved away, standing awkwardly in the middle of the living room, slowly removing her veil while Jake set a match to the peat fire. The roses on her headdress tumbled to the ground and she left them where they'd fallen on the worn carpet.

Her heart was thudding unnaturally and she kept telling herself that it was an odd situation, that anyone would feel uncomfortable under the circumstances. But there again there had been plenty of alliances like hers.

What did other couples do on the first night of their marriage of convenience? Play cards? Watch TV? And how did you bring up the subject of bed without sounding provocative? She ran her fingers through her hair distractedly. All that would come later. More difficulties. More tension.

First, though, there would be the revelation. One she'd had to be 'prepared' for. Maybe she wouldn't feel like doing anything afterwards, she thought gloomily.

Although she looked at him expectantly, Jake seemed in no hurry to unburden himself because all he did was give her a brief smile. Or, rather, he stretched his lips in the semblance of one. It seemed that he felt apprehensive too. Amber couldn't stand the strain.

'I'll get you that dram,' she muttered, and headed for the big dresser. 'Donald's brought your case up, I see. You could take it up. You have the room to the left.'

It seemed an odd thing to say to her husband. Feeling hollow with misery, she hid her face in the fall of her hair as she bent over the dresser and lifted out a couple of tumblers. One drink wouldn't hurt her child, she thought. And it would fortify her. Mercifully, Jake did as she suggested and she was left with time to pour their drinks shakily and compose herself.

It would help, she thought, if she was doing something when he came down again—something to occupy her hands that was placid and boring. The ironing might be disconcerting!

Then, as she wandered around restlessly, her eyes fell on the metal chest which sat on a sturdy table in the corner. The chest had been locked ever since her mother's death because she hadn't been able to face the memories stored in there—the photos, the letters, the memorabilia her mother had treasured.

A memory popped into her mind. When she'd been persuaded to go out to Africa, Stuart had pestered her for the key, saying that he'd sort through her mother's things. He'd been unusually insistent but...

She froze when she realised why. Maybe he had been anxious to find something that he knew her mother had kept.

Slowly, as if drawn by a magnet, she walked to the chest. From upstairs came the sound of Jake's door closing. The bang and the rattle of the latch woke her from her dream-like trance. Quickly she took the key from where she'd hidden it behind the shutter and slipped it into the padlock. Everything was very tidy, making her think wistfully of her brisk, neat mother.

A footfall told her that Jake had come into the room. 'Go ahead,' he said with quiet encouragement.

When she looked up she saw that his expression was solemn and watchful as though he knew that she was on the edge of some unpleasant discovery. Her pulses began to race and she made an effort to keep control of her emotions.

'What am I looking for?' she asked in a low voice.

He came up behind her. Close enough for her to feel his breath whispering on the lobe of her ear. 'Drink that,' he said gently, holding out one of the glasses of whisky she'd poured. 'You'll need it.'

She did. 'And now?' she asked, unable to stop herself from shaking.

The weight of his body came to rest against her back, as if he was afraid that she'd fall otherwise. Ignoring the trembling of her body, he reached past her to check through the bank receipts and statements, old letters and stacks of postcards, all tied up with string. She felt his tension and it frightened her.

'You're looking for your birth certificate,' he said quietly.

The air was plucked from her body as if she'd been catapulted into a brick wall. She swayed and Jake's arms came around her, cradling her, his cheek firm and re-assuring against hers. The room whirled as a blackness threatened to overwhelm her, and then it steadied again.

'Would that be it?' she rasped, and pointed to a large sealed envelope marked with her name.

Jake stretched forward and picked it up. 'You've never seen your birth certificate?' he asked curiously. 'Not even when you sent up for your passport?'

'No,' she answered, leaning back against him, grateful that he was there. Into her mind kept jumping the ob-vious reason why it might have been kept from her all these years. And she kept pushing the possibility away.

'When I applied for a passport,' she said rapidly, filling her mind with words, 'Mother said she'd lost the original certificate and would have to get a copy and send it on to the passport office for me. I asked for it afterwards—and she told me that . . . that Stuart had kindly agreed to keep it in his safe, with other family documents. So when . . . when we decided to get married, I asked him to find it and attach it to my request for the special licence.'

'Presumably Stuart only had the copy,' mused Jake, 'since he didn't have access to this box. I think this is the original, Amber.'

She stared at the envelope in dismay. 'My mother has never lied, to my knowledge. Why would she pretend she'd lost it?' she asked unhappily.

'Open the envelope. Look at it.'

'No!'

Instinctively she drew back harder against him. And he held her steady, his grip somehow giving her strength. She realised that Jake had tried to get her in the right frame of mind for this. Her teeth clenched. He'd thought that if she was in a fighting mood then she might be able to cope. But she didn't want to see what was on the certificate. Not now. Not ever.

'You have to,' he breathed in her ear.

'I don't! It's obvious that my parents and Stuart didn't want me to see it! They cared for me. What they've done has always been in my best interests.' She remembered what Jake had said about foster or adoptive parents sometimes deciding not to tell children about their background. It seemed that his comment—surely not an idle one—might be horribly apt in her case. 'Burn it!' she urged. 'I don't want to know—'

'Damn you, Amber!' snapped Jake. 'Look at it or I'll tell you what's on it!'

She slammed her hands over her ears. With another muttered curse, Jake all but dragged her to the sofa. Clamped hip to hip with him, his arm securely around her, she sat stony-faced and trembling while he angrily eased out the documents and put them on her lap.

'You have no right to force information on me,' she said, her voice shaking with emotion. 'I refuse to sully my parents' memory. I won't listen to you. I don't have to look. I don't want my life turned upside down.'

'It already is!' he said grimly.

She drew in a shuddering breath. 'No. Not irrevocably. I can cope with being pregnant by a man who never cared about me. I can cope with the emotional after-effects of my mother's death and the exhausting workload I took on in Africa. But not with anything that damages my relationship with my parents.'

'You can. Together we can cope with anything,' he said surprisingly. 'This affects both of us.' He turned her face to his and her heart missed a beat. There was a fierce tenderness in the dark wells of his velvety eyes which baffled and weakened her. 'Look at it—and the other documents too. I know you've had a rough time, Amber. I know you think you don't have the reserves of energy to cope with any more hassles. But you do,' he crooned. 'I'll make sure of that.'

'H-how?' she stammered nervously.

'Like this.'

His gentle smile eased into her like sunlight. She felt her heart thudding as he slipped the palm of his hand around the back of her scalp and continued to smile tenderly at her. Bewildered by her inability to draw away, she stared at him with confused eyes and frantically licked her parted lips so that she could say something clever.

She didn't have time. To her consternation, Jake was murmuring soothing words—appealingly soft, smouldering, lulling words. And she could feel herself yielding in his arms and settling into his embrace as if she was so desperate that she welcomed it with all her heart.

Her startled eyes were fixed on his beautifully sensual mouth while her mind struggled with the fact that a lyrical sensation was coursing through her appallingly defenceless body. She couldn't stop it…and didn't want to.

Then he kissed her. Amber stayed very still. It was so unlike anything she'd expected or had experienced before that she didn't move or breathe or respond for a long, long while. This time Jake's mouth was soft and as sweet as honey. As warm and as smooth as sun-kissed skin. It was beautiful. If they'd stayed locked like that for a day, she would have been cured of all her woes.

Guiltily postponing her indignation, she let herself lie back in his strong arms, savouring the wonderfully sensuous languor that was creeping through her body. And it wasn't a weakness that invaded her but a strength.

For the first time in her life a man was kissing her as if that was his sole aim. Miraculously, Jake didn't seem interested in moving on to the next step. His arms stayed around her securely, quite unthreatening. Their lips were parted but he was in no hurry to delve deeper. He was taking his time. A rare man indeed, she mused dreamily.

Then he drew back and gave her a gentle shake. 'Now you must look at the papers, Amber.'

'Jake?' she said wonderingly.

'Look at them!'

The colour soared up through her to stain her face a soft scarlet. He'd been totally in control of himself—and she'd temporarily lost her mind!

Her pearly white teeth snagged her lip. Reluctantly, she stared at the papers and waited for her eyes to focus because they seemed to be misty. Jake's arm was still around her shoulders and he gave her an encouraging squeeze as she read—and then reread—the first document, her birth certificate, with eyes as sharp as lasers now and her heart beating like an African drum.

'Dorothy *Elliott*? My mother was...Dorothy Elliott?' she whispered. 'But who...?' Her voice ended in a harsh croak. What did it matter who the woman was? She wasn't the same woman she'd called 'Mother'.

'Go on,' Jake said gently.

She took a long breath in. '"Dorothy Elliott, unemployed. Father...not known."' Those last words danced before her eyes. She was illegitimate. A groan escaped from her dry lips.

'You were adopted,' Jake said quietly. 'Angus and Elizabeth Fraser adopted you at birth from the Sunnyside Nursing Home, Glasgow.'

Jake had known. *Why* had he known? When? 'Who told you?' she demanded through her teeth. 'Stuart, I suppose!' Jake lowered his eyes and she couldn't see if her assumption was correct or not. 'Was it him?'

'I'm not prepared to answer that. I promised I wouldn't say,' he said gravely, still avoiding her eyes.

'It was Stuart!' she decided, hurt. 'Why did he tell you this? And why did you tell me?' she wailed. 'I didn't want to know! Everyone had kept the secret all these years and—and you had to blab it out—'

'You had to know. One day you would have sorted through your mother's things and you would have found out, Amber,' Jake said quietly.

Annoyingly, his logic was faultless. The facts would have come out sooner or later, though she wished that Jake had waited till she was stronger in herself. She felt beyond tears. Something cold and hard had taken up residence inside her—a protection, perhaps, now that her world seemed to be disintegrating piece by piece.

'Yes. I suppose you're right,' she admitted in a bitter monotone.

'Look, Amber—I think this was your natural mother,' Jake said gently.

Numb with shock, she turned questioningly to him. He held open a heavy silver locket. In it was a picture of a tense-looking blonde woman who seemed vaguely familiar, though perhaps that was wishful thinking. She was holding a newborn baby sporting a curly red quiff. The baby was unmistakably *her*.

'Oh, Jake!' she sighed, and held the locket in her trembling fingers, looking at it in a dazed fashion. Her fist closed over it as if to brand her mother's image into her body. 'Dorothy Elliott!' she said stupidly.

Unconsciously, she began to rock backwards and forwards, her fingers clenched over that locket as if she never wanted to release it. And, as if the sight of her true mother had unlocked a dam of emotion, she began to cry. Terrible sobs lurched out of her body—sobs that tore at her chest and hurt her throat.

'Hush, hush,' soothed Jake, pressing her head into his shoulder. 'Your baby—'

'Was conceived out of wedlock like me,' she said bitterly.

'Maybe you weren't—'

'Where's my father's name on my birth certificate?' she demanded hysterically. 'Tell me that!'

'There could be many explanations for its omission,' he argued.

'Oh, sure! My mother probably had so many boyfriends that she didn't know who my father was!'

'Maybe she was married but didn't want your father to know about your existence,' suggested Jake. When Amber gave a long, shuddering sob, he clasped her tightly and held her for a while, then whispered in her ear, 'Keep that courage high, Amber. Think of your health, your baby...'

'It's a little late to worry about that!' she mumbled. 'You decided to hurl a bomb into my already problematic life—'

'I had to,' he insisted.

'But *now*?'

'Yes. Now,' he said with a sigh of regret. 'Look, I don't like seeing you upset—'

'Then why do this to me?' she wailed, knowing that she was being unreasonable.

'I was the instrument, the messenger,' he said patiently. 'If it's anyone's fault, it's probably your father's.'

'Whoever he is,' she muttered. 'This is terrible. I can't believe I have no real tie with my parents. And they were everything to me! I feel . . . cheated.'

'They loved you as if you were their own child,' Jake murmured placatingly against her hair. 'They loved you so much that they couldn't bear you not to be theirs. Stuart did tell me that.'

He pressed his mouth to her forehead in a soothing kiss and snuggled her closer. Gratefully she let him comfort her. She needed him. Needed a kind, compassionate human being to help her get through this. A fresh frenzy of weeping racked her for a while and then she became aware that he was talking to her still.

'And as a child you were so utterly happy,' he was saying, 'and they couldn't bear to destroy your happiness. When you left for Africa Stuart was supposed to come and take the evidence away but you'd padlocked everything and he was far too mindful of your feelings to break in. He's been afraid of this for years.'

'Why?' she cried passionately, pulling away and gazing at Jake, her tear-stained face a picture of distress. 'Why shouldn't I have known about this when my mother— m-my adoptive mother—died?' she said.

'Oh, Amber!' Jake sighed. 'Stuart thought you'd prefer not to know. You said as much yourself. He knew how you'd feel.'

'But he told *you* . . .' Again she saw Jake look away, as if to hide the expression that lurked in his eyes. Frustrated, she said, 'It's perfectly clear that he did! You both argued about the wisdom of letting me know, didn't you?'

'We did.'

Her mind ran through the possible explanations. And she hit on one. 'He thinks we're in love,' she said in a small voice. Jake shifted as if he felt uncomfortable hearing that. 'I imagine he was afraid I'd open the chest and find out the truth one day when you were with me—and he thought you'd better know.' She fixed him with a direct look. 'He hoped you'd be able to comfort me, didn't he?'

'Actually, no. He wanted me to get the key and remove anything that referred to your natural mother. He didn't want to lose you, you see.'

Putting aside her shock at Stuart's uncharacteristically sly behaviour, Amber frowned and said, 'Lose me? What are you talking about?' Wordlessly, Jake handed her his handkerchief and she dabbed at her damp face in a perfunctory way. 'I wouldn't ever stop loving Stuart,' she argued. 'There's no reason for him to think I'd leave him either.'

There was a heavy silence and Amber filled it with her racing thoughts. Jake knew of a reason. Perhaps one that damned Stuart. There could only be one explanation. In sudden alarm, she dropped the handkerchief and grabbed Jake's arms fiercely. 'He—he's not my f-father, is he?' she stuttered. 'Stuart—?'

'No!' Jake's vehement denial was more than enough to convince her. 'No, Amber.' Several seconds passed and she waited in tense anticipation, willing Jake to expand. Eventually he did. 'Stuart was afraid you'd go looking for your natural parents.'

'I probably will.' She frowned, perplexed. 'But that won't take me away from Castlestowe and Stuart, will it?'

'It could.'

Amber shivered. 'Tell me,' she whispered, paling at Jake's solemn tone.

'These adverts explain it all.' The last remaining item on his lap was a card, onto which someone, presumably her mother, had pasted three newspaper cuttings. Jake passed this to her.

She read the first. '"Mandy Cook, née Brandon"—Brandon?' she cried in astonishment.

'Ignore it,' dismissed Jake. 'It's a false claim to the name. Nothing to do with the Brandons at all.'

'How do you know?' she asked suspiciously.

'Read on.' His expression showed that he wouldn't be drawn.

Although irritated, Amber's curiosity got the better of her and she bent her head to scan the cutting again. '"Brandon. Born 26.8.71, Sunnyside Nursing Home, Glasgow." Jake! This is where you said I was born! I'm not Mandy Cook, am I? I don't feel like a Mandy—'

'No. Continue.'

Shaking with tension, she did so. '"Resident of West Hill Children's Home, and St Mary's Children's Home. Married David James Cook, 26.8.89. Last heard of in Devon. Please contact the office below where you will learn something to your advantage."'

'Next.' His finger stabbed at the second advert.

The top line made her start and look up at Jake but he motioned her on so she read it all out in a breathless voice. '"Virginia Temple. Born 26.8.71, Sunnyside Nursing Home, Glasgow, subsequently 47 Barracks Lane. Last heard of at Lee Lane Women's Refuge, 1975, in the care of Sarah Temple ... Please contact the office below where you will learn something to your advantage."'

She went cold. 'It's the same nursing home, the same phone number, Jake.'

'Yes. Fifty miles away as the crow flies. The first child named in the advert has the surname of a well-known laird. The second is Virginia Temple, who was adopted and became Virginia McKenzie,' he said quietly. 'Ginny. Leo's Ginny.' Amber stared at him, speechless. 'The adverts were placed by Vincente St Honoré, who has been looking for his daughter. I told you about him, remember?'

Somehow she found her voice. 'You—you said he was an old man. And that he was dying. Something about owning a plantation which Ginny expects to inherit.'

Jake nodded slowly, watching her like a hawk. The rest of the news sank in and for a moment her mind went blank with shock. She and Ginny had been born in the same nursing home on the same day. Surely that was too great a coincidence?

Wincing because she'd been an unwanted baby, she became aware of Jake patiently waiting for some comment from her, and she stored away the connection she'd made till she could think it through.

His hand closed on hers. 'I had a chat with Leo. Vincente St Honoré has refused to let Ginny take a DNA test. That means either he's one hundred per cent sure Ginny is his daughter or he doesn't want to find out she isn't.'

She frowned, thinking that Jake was being unnecessarily suspicious. 'I don't see that it matters. What happened to St Honoré's wife?'

'She ran away.' Jake paused, and she had the impression that he was choosing his words carefully. 'I think I've already mentioned that Vincente has a dubious reputation. He treated his wife rather badly, moving his mistress into the house. Rumour suggests that his wife suffered physical abuse too.'

'Does Leo know this?' she cried in alarm.

Jake nodded. 'He says there's no truth in the rumours and Vincente has been misunderstood.' His caustic ex-

pression and tone made it clear what he thought of that.
'However, the facts speak for themselves. Madame St
Honoré ran away because she couldn't take any more.
She was pregnant but Vincente didn't know till he read
the note she'd left him. And by then she had disap-
peared off the face of the earth.'

'He sounds thoroughly unpleasant,' she said,
wrinkling her nose with disgust. 'Poor Ginny, to have a
father like him!'

Jake grunted in agreement. 'Vincente decided to trace
his child when he discovered he was dying. The detective
agency he employed came up with three names. There
were three women who'd given birth in the right place
at the right time. One of them had to be his child. Mandy
was the first to answer the advert but the DNA test elim-
inated her. When Ginny met Vincente, however, he said
she was the image of his wife.'

'I'm not sure whether to be happy for her or sad,'
Amber said ruefully. 'But I'm sure Leo can look after
her.'

Jake slanted his eyes at her. 'Read the last advert.'

It was much the same as the others. But this time the
person being sought was...Amber Elliott. Daughter of
Dorothy Elliott. Her eyes sought Jake's uneasily. Three
women, who'd given birth in the right place at the right
time. One of them her own natural mother. 'Extraordinary,' she said faintly.

Jake frowned at the creases in the knees of his trousers
and smoothed them down, saying, 'Investigators traced
the man who sheltered Madame St Honoré when she
fled to Britain. He has confirmed that Ginny is Vincente
St Honoré's daughter.'

That let her off the hook! Relieved, Amber smiled. It
was a romantic story, despite the fact that the plantation
owner sounded the last person *she'd* want as a father.

'He'd know, wouldn't he? That settles it for Ginny and Leo, then,' she said warmly.

Jake gave a sardonic smile. 'But the man lied,' he said with soft intensity.

Inexplicably, her pulses quickened. 'Why—why would he do that?' She gulped. There was a look of pity in his eyes.

'To protect someone.'

'Madame St Honoré?' she suggested. He shook his head, still looking at her with a sad tenderness which made her cast around for an explanation.

And finally it seemed that everything dropped into place. Amber knew why Jake had led her, step by laborious step, to this point. By simple elimination he believed that *she* was St Honoré's daughter.

CHAPTER FOUR

AMBER sat in stunned silence. She felt Jake's arm slip from her shoulder and she wanted to beg him to stay but she seemed incapable of speech or movement. When he left her she felt quite bereft, as if she'd begun to need him already, just as he'd predicted. A shiver went right through her and she tried not to feel that way but knew that she did need him to comfort her and nothing would change that, whatever she told herself.

There were sounds in the kitchen of a kettle being filled, cupboards being opened, a teapot and cups rattling. Tea! she thought in a great sweep of relief. Jake would be coming back in a moment. They'd be able to talk this through.

She closed her eyes to hold back her anguish as she dwelt on the thought that Vincente St Honoré might be her father. If Jake's information was right—and it usually was—the planter was an obnoxious man, brutal and amoral... Her involuntary shudder at the contrast between the planter and her father lanced through her chest. Angus Fraser had always had a cheerful smile for everyone. They'd all admired his straight-as-a-die character and the love he'd borne her and... Amber bit her lip and corrected herself. And her *adoptive* mother.

Calling them her adoptive parents seemed like a betrayal. To all intents and purposes Elizabeth and Angus had been her parents in everything but blood. What made someone a mother or a father anyway? A cluster of genes, chains of DNA, inherited diseases, hair colour, body types? That part was easy. Nowadays it could even be accomplished via a test-tube.

But what Angus and Elizabeth had achieved was more difficult. They had given her such a loving environment that she had never doubted for a moment that she was their own dearly loved daughter.

Amber's soft mouth became firm with decision. She wouldn't deny them. To her they were her parents, not the two strangers who'd created her. And she didn't want to risk finding out that Vincente and Madame St Honoré—or Dorothy Elliott, as she'd apparently called herself—were those two strangers. Especially Vincente.

'I made some tea,' Jake said unnecessarily, coming in with the tray.

'Thanks.' She looked up with pleading eyes and he read their message, coming to sit with her again. And she felt better for the return of his company.

For a moment there was silence while Jake slipped the pair of heavy gold cuff-links from his cuffs, rolled up his shirtsleeves and jerked at his bow-tie till it came undone. Then he eased open the top button of his dress shirt in a gesture that she found disturbingly sexy despite the tense situation, and flung his arm along the back of the sofa, his scrutiny of her unusually probing.

'Had any thoughts?' he asked carefully.

Amber's edginess came out in a rush of words. 'Yes! I want to pretend I know nothing about this! Ginny's happy. I assume Vincente's happy. Leo too, and Stuart. Let's leave it at that, Jake!' she cried, her expression desperate.

Soothingly he touched her cheek and let his fingers rest on her soft skin. 'No, Amber. We can't.'

Mentally she shook away the pacifying effect of his fingertips. She didn't want to be placated or persuaded to accept his way of thinking. 'Why not?' she demanded. 'You could be wrong when you say that this man is lying. What evidence do you have to doubt his word, anyway?'

'Tell me,' said Jake gravely, idly drawing his fingers downwards to her jaw. 'In my work, what am I known for?'

Without any conscious decision on her part, her lips parted as she felt the warmth of the sweeping caress stimulating her skin and the millions of nerve-endings which seemed to be leaping to his touch.

'Compassion.' Amber blinked at the answer she'd blurted out hastily to divert herself from the quickening of her pulses. It was true. Everyone regarded Jake as a very empathetic and humanitarian man.

He smiled faintly. 'And?'

This, she thought ruefully, was fast on the way to becoming a list of qualities she regarded highly in a man. And it seemed a little unwise to admit how well he matched up to her personal standards. With a frown of reluctance, she shrugged to minimise any suggestion that she also admired him.

'Integrity, so they say.'

'How kind of them,' he said gravely, his fingers hovering unnervingly close to the corner of her mouth. 'And?'

She tore her attention away from the maddening sensation of each invasive finger and scowled. 'OK,' she said grudgingly, 'the ability to expose the truth.' Knowing that it was more than that, she decided to risk pandering to his vanity. She might as well be hanged for a sheep as a lamb. 'You're known for your sixth sense and the way you identify plausible liars and trip them up with their own words,' she admitted.

'I was hoping you'd say something like that. So you accept my judgement?'

She shrugged again. 'Your track record speaks for itself. If you suspect this man of ulterior motives in saying Ginny is Vincente's daughter, then I have to believe you for the moment, since I don't have any evidence to counter it,' she said slowly. 'But why, Jake? You said he was protecting someone...but surely that isn't all? What would the man gain?'

The black and compelling eyes were briefly veiled. It might have been deliberate or it might have been because he intended to pour the tea. She wasn't sure. Jake set her cup in front of her and then leaned back again and cuddled her into his shoulder, his breath sweet and warm on her face.

Perhaps she could have objected. Though it would have seemed churlish, she told herself. Especially as his embrace was more than welcome. Although her mind whirled with fears and worries, she felt strangely secure. Jake's body was warm beneath the crispness of the shirt, and densely muscled. It gave her a good feeling.

'My gut instincts, and the information I've gathered, tell me that this man stands to gain quite a lot,' Jake said softly.

'Money?' she hazarded, her skirts rustling as she shifted around a little to half face him.

'Not money,' he said reassuringly. 'The guy's doing it for his own needs, I think. Until I'm certain, I'd prefer not to say anything. But I don't think we can ignore what we know. Maybe you're not St Honoré's daughter. But there is an element of doubt—and you must at least persuade Leo that Ginny should take the DNA test.'

'It might cause a lot of heartache,' she demurred, lifting her thick lashes to look up at him. 'I'd rather do nothing.'

Jake's eyes narrowed. 'Then I would have to present my evidence without your help.'

Amber stiffened. 'You don't want me to have a choice at all!' she complained vigorously.

'No,' he admitted evenly.

Her eyes flashed with annoyance. 'Don't you think that's unfair? Shouldn't I be the one who judges whether this should go any further? Why are you so insistent about this, Jake?'

'Because truth will always out,' he said grimly. 'Leo and Ginny could commit themselves to the old man and the plantation, spending time and money and emotional energy there, only to be evicted by a close relative who's proved that Ginny has no blood link. I'm told Vincente has a sister who has ambitions for her son. I doubt she'd stand by and let the family inheritance go to Ginny without incontrovertible proof.'

Amber grimaced and subsided. 'Oh. I hadn't realised. Then I agree; I must persuade Leo to get that proof.'

'Good,' murmured Jake. But she'd seen the flicker of triumph in his eyes and was worrying about it. 'I'll leave you to speak to Leo when we go to St Lucia.'

Her head jerked up. No wonder Jake had been certain she'd go to St Lucia with him! And presumably his choice of honeymoon hide-away hadn't been chance. Jake had carefully manoeuvred her where he wanted her. A master strategist. The question was why?

'What if Ginny isn't the planter's daughter?' she asked quietly.

Jake's hand absently soothed the back of hers. 'We'll cross that bridge when we come to it.'

Detaching herself temporarily from Jake's arms, she leaned forward and took a few sips of her tea, nursing the cup in her hands and staring absently into the fire. Despite his apparently casual manner, he was very tense.

'You've made some elaborate plans. Why are you doing this, Jake?' she asked warily.

'You know me. I hear of something, it intrigues me, I follow it to the bitter end—'

'It's more than that.' His light tone hadn't fooled her at all.

He smiled crookedly, a gentle affection softening his face. 'I believe strongly in justice, Amber. Perhaps obsessively. And,' he said, taking her hand and staring into her eyes, 'I have a personal interest in this. There's a chance that you're Vincente's daughter. You ought to know, one way or the other. You and your child could stand to inherit his plantation and I want to help you find out the truth.'

'That's kind of you,' she said gratefully. 'But I'm not sure I want to know. I thought when we were married I'd have a quieter life. It seems I'm being flung back into the maelstrom.'

Jake's hand moved to rest squarely on her back in a gesture of comfort. 'At least this time you can jump in on your own terms. If you ignore this now, I'm convinced that one day you'll find yourself catapulted into the thick of trouble whether you like it or not. By taking your own steps at your own pace you stay in charge— you do as much as you want, when you want. And remember,' he said, 'I'll be with you every step of the way.'

'Will you, Jake?' she asked, reluctantly swayed by his eloquent eyes.

'I promise,' he said softly. 'And if you do want to know about your natural mother then I'll move heaven and earth to find her for you.'

Overwhelmed, she put down the cup and turned to him. His hand slipped to grasp hers as she stared at him with enormous, soulful eyes.

'Thank you, Jake. You're being very kind to me again,' she said in a small voice. And she pleaded silently,

Please don't let him be false. Please let me feel I can put my trust in him and let it be justified!

'I want to help you. I want to put your mind at rest.' The darkness of his eyes drew her in. They were warm and affectionate so she smiled hesitantly and was rewarded with his dazzling, crooked grin. 'Sleep on it. Let your subconscious mind do the work and we'll talk further in the morning,' he advised huskily.

'I will,' she sighed, passing a tired hand through her hair. 'I'm so tired, my head's dizzy.'

Jake lightly stroked her furrowed brow till the lines were ironed out. 'I don't think we'll forget our wedding day in a hurry!' he said ruefully, and they both laughed, then his face went serious. 'Amber...don't be worried about going to St Lucia tomorrow,' he said. 'We can come home whenever you want.'

'Home,' she repeated wistfully, remembering his threat. It *had* been an empty taunt, hadn't it? 'That will be Castlestowe, won't it?' she asked, ready to defy anything to the contrary.

'If you want it to be.' He looked contrite. 'I'm sorry I used your love of your home to raise your fighting spirit. I was alarmed when I saw how weary you seemed. I knew what lay ahead and that you'd need to be strong to face the revelations about your parents. I couldn't think of any other way to snap you out of your mood.'

'It was brutal.'

'I apologise. I honestly don't care where I live,' Jake explained. 'I have no special roots of my own.'

'You didn't like Kenya?' she asked in surprise.

He was silent for a while. Imperceptibly his hand tightened and she realised that he didn't know how hard he was squeezing her fingers. Biting her lip, Amber waited for him to tell her what had made him look so grim.

'My childhood home has some painful memories.'
Jake brooded on the threadbare patch of the rug at his
feet. 'Someone died. Someone I loved very much. Suddenly the sun, the carefree life, the sheer joy of living—
all those things meant nothing any more. I was twenty-
three and it seemed that my life was meaningless. Everywhere I went seemed to be full of memories and I found
that unbearable. So I left and never returned.'

Amber wanted to reach out and touch his hurt face.
But all she did was keep silent and steel herself against
the pain of her crushed hand. It must have been a very
deep, very passionate relationship, she thought. True
love. It explained a great deal.

'I started my lifetime of wandering then,' Jake continued in a barely audible voice. 'Caroline...'

He was so choked up that he couldn't go on. Her heart
went out to him as he stared and stared at the rug, his
chest heaving with pent-up emotion.

'Caroline,' she said with infinite compassion.

Jake started, his breath shooting out in a hiss as he
nodded and visibly began to gain control of himself
again. 'I feel so bitter about her death. I thought I'd
overcome my feelings but I was wrong. They've been
resurrected again and I'll never forget.'

'I see.' And now she knew where she stood. He would
love Caroline for ever. A short while ago that would
have reassured her. Now it made her feel sad.

'I'm not sure you do. Perhaps if I tell you what happened you'll understand why your plight touched me so
much, Amber,' he said quietly. There was a pause while
he prepared to say something which she imagined he'd
never voiced before. 'When I knew about your situation, I had a sense of *déjà vu*. You see, Caroline got
mixed up with someone with a doubtful reputation. And
he got her pregnant.'

It was blindingly clear. Amber's mouth thinned. He'd married her out of pity, as a kind of tribute to the memory of the woman he'd loved. 'Oh!' she breathed, feeling oddly hollow and forlorn. 'I—I'm sorry,' she said, with an effort.

Jake frowned at her white-knuckled hand and hastily loosened his grip, gently massaging her fingers till they looked more normal. 'Did I do that? I didn't mean to hurt you.'

'That's all right, Jake,' she said, her face sad. 'I do understand a little more about you now and I'm grateful to you for telling me.' There was a silence for a while. 'I'm scared,' she admitted. 'Suddenly there's the possibility that I might have lost everything I built my life on.'

'I don't think that's true,' he countered. 'Your childhood was idyllic and the Frasers loved you. You'll never forget, never lose those memories. And there's no reason for you to be worried about your home. Stuart has said that your cottage is yours for as long as you want it.'

Her eyes filled with tears. He was right. She had nothing to lose by going to St Lucia and persuading Ginny that it was in her own interests to establish her right to St Honoré's plantation. Even if the test proved negative, thought Amber, she needn't have anything to do with Vincente if she didn't want to.

'Thank you, Jake,' she said, overcome with emotion. And on an impulse she reached up and lightly kissed his smiling mouth.

She was stricken with a great urge to let her lips linger, because they fitted his so beautifully. She felt a desire to crush his mouth beneath hers, to drive out all fears and forebodings with sheer physical intensity. Fortunately, he drew back before she could make such an abject fool of herself.

'Take your tea and go to bed. I'll see you in the morning,' he said gruffly.

Amber rose to her feet, a little hurt that he'd dismissed her so abruptly. 'Night,' she mumbled.

'You'll be all right?'

Surprised, she shot him a quick look and saw that he really was concerned for her welfare. 'Yes,' she said, flashing him a bright smile, and walked out before he saw the tears of relief gathering in her eyes. He cared. He really cared about her.

And, although she'd had several shocks during the last hour or so, her heart seemed to lift and she felt more confident about his motives. She was almost certain that she could trust him. Almost.

Dawn was breaking as she closed the curtains and then slipped into bed in her new satin nightdress—a gift from one of her bridesmaids and part of the bridal ritual she'd blindly followed. But although the material felt beautifully smooth and sensuous against her skin she couldn't sleep. Her mind just whirled and whirled and she went over and over the things Jake had said.

For a long time she tossed and turned and counted sheep. Finally she gave up and crossly sat up, deciding to go downstairs and fix herself a drink of hot chocolate. And some oatcakes, she thought, feeling ravenously hungry. At the wedding she'd been so nervous that she'd eaten nothing.

Eager to make a snack, she reached for the matching satin robe and then hesitated. The candlewick dressing gown, a faded pink and with barely any 'wick' left, would be warmer and more practical. She put it on and gazed in fascinated horror at her reflection. She couldn't.

She just *couldn't* wear it, even if Jake was dead to the world and snoring his head off!

'Oh, vanity!' she sighed, knowing that she'd freeze and would pay for her stupidity if she tripped down in thin satin. So she tied the belt of the pink candlewick gown and avoided looking at herself again.

And she almost ran back upstairs when she saw Jake sprawled on the sitting-room floor in front of the banked-up fire. It was obvious that he hadn't even attempted to sleep, because he still wore his dress shirt and trousers, though his shoes had been slipped off and the shirt had been unbuttoned a little further.

Amber politely averted her eyes from the disturbing breadth of male chest that had been exposed and smiled ruefully when he caught sight of her where she hesitated in the doorway. To his credit, he didn't even blink at the dreadful dressing gown. He put down his mug of coffee and smiled.

'Oh, dear!' she exclaimed, a little breathlessly. 'You too!'

'Me too.'

There was something unnervingly intimate about the way he spoke. She averted her gaze from his indolent eyes and said stupidly, 'I couldn't sleep!'

'I'm not surprised. Here.' He patted the floor beside him. 'Human comfort. We both need it.' Tempting, thought Amber, hesitating nevertheless. 'Why don't you get a hot drink and keep me company?' suggested Jake quietly, his expression suddenly bleak. His eyes bored into her soul. 'I seem to have bitten off more than I can chew.'

'Oh, Jake!' she cried in a rush of compassion, and hurried over to settle by his side. 'I'm sorry! You've given up so much for me... You've been flung into a complicated situation and you've done everything you can to make things easy for me... I do appreciate it,' she said earnestly, laying her hand on his arm. 'I appreciate your thoughtfulness and your concern. If this has done nothing else, it's proved to me that we'll get on well together.'

'I've always known that, Amber,' he answered. And, as if by mutual consent, she settled happily in his arms. 'We've had some laughs together, haven't we?' he mused.

'I'm surprised you didn't laugh at my appearance right now,' she said wryly.

'Laugh?' he repeated, puzzled. His head angled to one side and she quivered at the lustrous depth of his eyes. 'I think you look utterly beautiful, Amber.'

A pulsing huskiness overlaid his voice. It slowed her brain and softened her body. 'In pink candlewick?' she managed to scoff.

'In pink candlewick.'

She swallowed nervously. Things were getting out of hand. 'You have appalling taste, Jake Cavendish!' she said lightly. 'I'll never ask you to help me choose clothes.'

'You do all right on your own,' he said admiringly. 'I have a vivid memory of you wearing an electric-blue dress in Sarajevo and cutting a swathe through official red tape because of it!'

'I did?' she said in confusion. 'I didn't know...' Her voice became a croak. Jake was absently tracing the lines on her palm. Sharp twinges of deliciously wicked feelings were shooting through her. Hastily she withdrew her hand and took a sip of his coffee.

'Relax,' he murmured drily. 'I'm not going to jump you.'

'Oh! You're not?' she blurted out, startled by his remark.

'Do you want me to?'

'No!'

Jake laughed and she did too, though not so heartily. He went to get a blanket and wrapped her in it. 'There,' he said, standing up, apparently amused by the sight of her face emerging from the huge woollen cocoon. 'Out of sight, out of mind. Or so they say.'

He leaned down to plant a light kiss on her nose. His face hovered an inch or so away from hers and her wicked inner self begged, pleaded with him to kiss her on the mouth. Her lips even opened in a provocative pout which caused Jake to frown and walk over to gaze out of the window, his shoulders unnaturally high where they were silhouetted against the brightness of the morning outside.

'Friends,' he said tightly. 'That's all. Yes?' he shot at her, turning abruptly on his heel to face her.

Miserably she nodded and lowered her head in shame at his polite but pointed rebuke. She'd gone too far and had mistaken his interest.

Worse, her feelings for Jake were confused. He *was* sexy. She *did* feel physically attracted to him—she couldn't help it. But she'd humiliated herself once over her sexual response to a man. It would be dreadful if she allowed that to happen again.

What she was beginning to feel for Jake was something else entirely. She brooded over this. A fatal fascination. No, more than that. She felt happy to be with him. A liking for him had always been there, from the very beginning. Then had come admiration, both for his expertise and his love for humanity. Now...every time he held her she felt a deep glow. Somehow he promoted an inner peace within her and her worries were lessened.

But she mustn't fall for him, however lovable he might seem. He pitied her but he didn't love her and it was unlikely that he ever would. That was her tragedy. Trapped in a loveless marriage. Half in love with a

husband who wanted only to be her friend. What had
she done? What *had* she done?

'Amber,' he said in soft reproach.

Inexplicably, she lowered her head to her knees and
began to cry. Terrible, body-racking sobs heaved painfully from her body. In an instant Jake was at her side,
embracing her, crushing her in his arms. That made it
worse. She found herself howling into his shoulder till
her tears had saturated his shirt.

And he rocked her—she, a touchingly shapeless bundle
of misery in the enveloping blanket, her eyes red and
swollen when he stopped to wipe them with his handkerchief, her face washed with salty tears.

'I'm s-s-sorry!' she sobbed. 'I don't know why I'm
crying!'

'It's OK. Understandable. Hush,' he said gruffly,
kissing her eyelids.

'I feel ... overwhelmed.' She sniffed, casting around
for a reason to explain her misery.

'Of course you do.' His mouth pressed consolingly on
her damp temple.

'Enzo's rejection ... my tiredness, the sickness ...'

'Yes. But you're all right now. I'm here.'

Bliss stole over her. Jake was with her. She snuggled
deeper into his arms. 'Oh, Jake!' she sighed.

And suddenly their lips met; whether she made the
first move or he she didn't know; she only knew that
her heart was soaring and her tears had miraculously
stopped. His hands held her face gently as his mouth
locked to hers, dizzyingly coaxing passion from the
depths of her very heart.

His mouth pressed on her closed eyelids again, the
sensation of warmth making her sigh. Sweetly, tenderly
he kissed her face, inch by inch, and she responded by
kissing the warm, honeyed smoothness of his skin, her

fingers exploring the contrasting rasp where a faint stubble curved along his jaw.

'Jake...'

'Amber,' he growled urgently under his breath.

He sounded shaken—a fact which ignited her passion and caused her to groan and offer up her yielding mouth, her throat, the sensitive area below her small ears. Tenderly Jake lifted back her heavy hair and ardently savoured the places where her pulse beat while an exploratory hand slipped past the barriers of blanket, dressing gown and satin to the smooth warmth of her breast.

Silent and intense, he stared at her as the peak became suddenly taut. She could feel its roused point throbbing for attention beneath his stilled hand and felt an unbearable sense of waiting. His eyes asked a question. Hers answered. In response, he carefully drew apart the edges of the blanket and her robe and sat staring at her, his eyes drowsy with need and an undisguised admiration that thrilled her.

His eyes closed briefly and then he leaned forward, his hands gently slipping down the satin straps of her nightdress. She had never felt so elated in the whole of her life. Delirium made her bold. Emotion welled up in her heart and spilled out recklessly.

Her hands lifted in a graceful motion, drawing his head to her breast, and she gave a little shudder as his lips parted then closed over her long, hard nipple. 'Oh-h-h-h!' she moaned, willing him to go on and on and on...

Gently, decisively he pushed her to the floor. His tongue flickered and teased at her heavy breasts and she began to lose control. Hazily she fumbled with the buttons of his shirt till she could place her palms on his beautiful chest and revel in the strong muscles, the dark, curling hairs which wound a fascinating path that disappeared beneath his waistband.

Her eyes darkened. He was drawing the satin nightdress down her body and pressing kisses on each new portion of skin that he exposed. With tender, loving hands, she stroked his silky black hair and bent forward to kiss his scalp, his forehead, his temples.

She felt an increased urgency in the touch of his hands and mouth. The satin was sliding more slowly but Jake's breathing was harsher. At her hips the soft material rested in tantalisingly sensuous folds. Again she felt an electrifying tug at her breasts which sent deep waves of sensation through her.

His mouth claimed hers. Warm, brutally hesitant, driving her crazy with its restraint. Tormented, she whimpered in her throat. Struggled to undo his belt. Muttered in frustration when the buckle refused to budge. And her fingers stilled because Jake was easing off her nightdress, sliding it seductively down her thighs till it was a small, luxurious heap at her feet, and then he was ripping at his belt as if demons possessed him.

Naked against his half-clothed body, she felt a shock of intense abandon. Her nipples just touched his skin and when he shifted his position they dragged dizzyingly across his chest till she felt that she would melt inside with wanting.

Passionate kisses sated her panting mouth and his arms closed around her as if he never wanted to let her go. This was lovemaking as she'd always longed for it to be. Slow, sensual, beautifully excruciating. She was intoxicated. Drunk from his mouth, the intuitive knowledge that he'd be good to her.

And yet he would treat her like a living, breathing, wanton woman.

The weakness intensified as his hands stole to her buttocks, moulding them in his palms, massaging them with a hard, quick rhythm that matched the growing demand of her body.

They fitted together. They moved as if they'd been choreographed. Their hearts beat with the same rapid thunder, their mouths met and parted, murmured and sighed. And his passion was hers. His need was identical to hers.

They tumbled about the floor, their arms and legs wrestling to imprison one another. And she knew in a terrible moment of discovery that the feelings she had for Jake were rooted in love. And with that discovery came total need.

He must have felt that imperceptible shift from uncertainty to pliant submission. Perhaps he saw something in her melting eyes that he didn't want to see. Because he went very still and then moved away, the spell of blissful silence broken.

Bewildered, she struggled to sit up, her movements ungainly because her body was refusing to obey. Jake was angrily pushing his arms into his shirtsleeves. 'What...?'

He was resolutely ignoring her. She gulped and grabbed the faded candlewick dressing gown, drawing it over her nakedness. Suddenly it seemed indecent. Her huge eyes watched as he scowled and wrestled with his buttons.

'I forgot. I apologise. I can't tell you how much I regret... I take the blame,' he growled savagely. 'I've been trying to ignore the effect you have on me all evening. I thought I'd succeeded but when I held you in my arms I couldn't help myself. I had to kiss you. And then... I couldn't stop. It was like a fever inside me, Amber!' He flashed her a dark, raw look.

She quivered with the intensity of his need.

'Oh.' It was all she could manage. She had no breath for anything else.

'I knew how emotional you were feeling,' he muttered. 'I pushed you over the edge. I shouldn't have done that. It was unforgivable.' He seemed to expect a comment.

'Mmm.' Amber blushed.

'The doctor told you to—be careful.' His voice was jerky and stilted. 'He said that with the restricted diet you'd had at the camp and the stress you'd suffered you were at a critical stage of your pregnancy.'

Her eyes closed. She'd forgotten. For one, glorious moment she'd felt like a desirable woman again. 'Yes. I am.' For the next two weeks or so, she thought bleakly. 'I thought...' She couldn't tell him what she'd thought. Her only hope of salvaging her self-respect was to retreat behind a barrier of excuses for her response. 'I was miserable. I couldn't help crying. You kissed me and...'

'Yes,' he said curtly, mercifully saving her from making the explanation. 'I know. You were vulnerable and I took advantage of that. You looked so damn kissable, Amber, and I'm only human!' he said with a touch of asperity.

Not human enough, she thought bitterly. Now she was left with a terrible ache and a feeling of deep embarrassment. Their situation wasn't clear-cut any longer. Somehow they had to live together and she'd need to decide whether she wanted their marriage to become normal in every way or not. It was a decision she'd rather not face at the moment.

'Do you know what you've done to me?' she mumbled.

'Yes,' he replied simply. And then he looked at her, took in her anguished eyes and sad mouth, the tremble

of her hands as she held the robe protectively against
her body. 'I've hurt you and made your trust in me falter.
It must seem as if I've thought of you only as a sex
object. It's not like that, Amber.'

'Isn't it?' Forlorn and unhappy, her whole body reproached him for tuning into her desire for love.

'No, it isn't. I see you as someone very special.' The
softness of his tone vibrated within her and she felt her
bones melt again, filling with a hopelessness that brought
tears of despair to her eyes. 'Our relationship is an odd
one,' he went on. 'We need time to let it grow, Amber.
You are the kind of woman a man could dream about.
Loving and sweet, intensely passionate, guileless.' He
knelt beside her like a lover. 'I'd hoped that in time our
friendship could become something closer...'

'Like...what?' she prompted softly.

Twin fringes of black lashes hid his eyes briefly and
he seemed to struggle for words. 'Like a really strong
bond,' he said at last, disappointing her. And she sensed
that he was wary of making any more of a commitment.
'Based on trust and mutual respect. My intention was
to look after you and make you happy. I thought we
might gently, slowly...'

'Yes?' She was holding her breath, wishing, hoping...

'I thought that one day we might feel like sharing more
than the same house.'

Presumably he was hoping they'd share a bed. He
wanted everything from her but love; he hadn't, perhaps
couldn't mention that all-important word. Amber looked
at his bowed head, fighting the urge to say that she'd
share her heart one day if he'd only surrender a little
portion of his.

'I see.'

He looked up and lifted his shoulders in a helpless
shrug. 'I know you won't want to think about that now.

I feel I've ruined everything,' he growled. 'I never intended to rush you so crudely.'

It hadn't been crude. Sudden, maybe. But his love-making had flowed like a smooth river, as if it was the most natural thing in the world for them to be yielding to one another.

'We were both overwrought,' she said huskily, close to tears again.

'I wanted you. I wanted to hold you and...' He frowned and lowered his head again. When he raised it, she found her gaze fixed by his and it wrung her heart to see him so pained. 'There are many things I want from you: physical passion, surrender... But they're nothing compared with my need to be trusted and liked by you, for our marriage to be strong and permanent. I won't be so crass as to risk our relationship again just because you're looking particularly irresistible.' He gave her a crooked grin. 'Forgive me.'

Somehow she managed to look away. There was hope. He wanted her friendship and for their marriage to be good. And he had found her irresistible. Time might bring love. One day he might get over the tragedy of his old love affair and be free to love again.

'Yes,' she husked on an outward breath. And with it went any remaining energy. Suddenly she felt totally drained.

Tenderly Jake took her hand and kissed it. 'Thank you, Amber.'

The room was radiant with sunlight by now but her eyes were closing and her limbs felt heavy. 'I'm so tired,' she muttered sleepily. As she slipped towards semi-consciousness she knew that Jake had taken her in his arms, but she was too exhausted to remonstrate with him.

'Sleep. I'll wake you in good time to get ready for the drive to the airport,' he murmured in her ear.

Her thoughts were further away than the Caribbean. They lingered in a make-believe world where she and Jake had grown closer, where they turned to one another for love and companionship and where he declared his love for her day after day with every breath in his body, every look in his eyes.

A dream world, she thought wistfully. She smiled and imagined that she felt his lips, warm on her mouth. Dreams could come true, she thought muzzily. She'd do everything in her power to ensure that this dream became real, for the sake of herself and her child.

Sighing, she turned in his arms and half woke to feel herself being held very tightly, Jake's heart thudding against her breast.

She'd capture that heart. Or break hers in the attempt.

CHAPTER FIVE

'YOU'RE like your old self,' Jake observed idly three weeks later as they were lounging on the veranda of Flame Trees, the mansion he'd rented in St Lucia.

Neither of them had been in a hurry to visit Ginny. It hadn't even been mentioned. Somehow it had seemed more important to re-establish their relationship—and for Amber to gain health and strength.

'And what is my old self?' asked Amber in secret delight. She knew perfectly well what he meant but she wanted him to say it. *Alive. Happy.*

He raised his glass of frosted daiquiri in a smiling toast. 'The woman I met,' he said, his eyes warm with memories, 'on the road to Bucharest. Your hire car was in a ditch, you were covered in oil and changing the wheel— and you were laughing.'

'Well, it was funny!' she said with a giggle. 'I was intending to arrive, change into something madly efficient and make an impression on my new boss— Mary—and this glamorous Reuters correspondent who was going to interview us both that evening.' Sliding Jake a puzzled glance, she said, 'Incidentally, I never knew why you did the interview instead of the journalist I was expecting. What happened to him?'

Jake studied his drink as he swirled the fruit around idly. 'Something came up for him and I took over,' he said lightly. 'These things happen all the time. When you didn't arrive, Mary was worried so I went out to find you—'

'And discovered a grubby female in a ditch!'

He smiled. 'I'll never forget it. You wore an emerald-green T-shirt and a skirt the colour of autumn leaves and your hair was tumbled about your face. Knockout. I wanted to grab you and kiss you then and there!'

'I never knew that!' she exclaimed, astonished and flattered that he could recall what she'd been wearing. 'You were very polite,' she mused. 'Almost too correct...'

'I had to be,' he said, chuckling. 'My basic instinct was to pin you against the car and kiss you breathless, so I had to get a grip. There's something very sexy about a woman who laughs in the face of adversity—and,' he said teasingly, 'who has a smudge of oil on her neat little nose.'

Amber beamed. The days they'd spent together had transformed their behaviour towards one another. On the neutral ground of Flame Trees they'd whiled away the time, enjoying the privacy of the grand colonial mansion and its extensive grounds. To her delight, the estate lay on the eastern side of the island, miles from the airport and the tourist areas. And in the warm sunshine their relationship had flourished as she'd hoped it would.

It was an idyllic setting and that had helped to ease their way. Flame Trees lay inland, beyond the golden sands and rock-enclosed coves on the windward coast where the sea crashed against the shore with as much ferocity as it did at Castlestowe, giving her that sense of wildness she loved in a landscape.

'I do remember that you got out your handkerchief and rubbed my nose for ages,' she said happily, returning to reminiscing about their first meeting. 'But you scowled like anything while you did it! Then you hardly spoke on the drive back and were very formal during the interview. I asked Mary about you when I reported for duty the next morning, you know.'

He flashed her a quick glance. 'Oh, yes?'

She grinned. He was so obviously trying not to sound interested! 'I asked her if you were always bad-tempered. She spent half an hour telling me you were a cross between the angel Gabriel and Lancelot and I wondered why such a paragon of virtue should have taken an instant dislike to me!'

Jake stretched out his legs on the lounger in contentment. 'Mary gave me a similar lecture six months later, when we all met up again,' he admitted. 'According to her, you were an invaluable member of the team and she intended to take you everywhere with her. I had the impression that you were very special.' He gave her a sideways look. 'She... loves you, I think, Amber.'

Amber's sweet smile lit her face. 'I hope that's true,' she said softly, conjuring up the image of the tall, stately woman with her neat cap of iron-grey hair. 'Mary guided me and helped me in everything I did for Unite. She's devoted her life to the organisation. I admire her enormously.'

'You talked to her a lot, didn't you?' he mused.

'Oh, she loved to hear my stories about my godfather and Castlestowe, about my parents and village life in Scotland. I think she gets a bit homesick for Britain, you know,' Amber confided. 'She never goes back. I caught her looking distinctly damp-eyed a couple of times.'

'And are *you* homesick?' he asked, a slight tension lifting his shoulders.

'No,' she said quickly. 'I do like it here—'

'As much as Castlestowe?'

'No, Jake!' She laughed at his disappointment. 'Never that. But Flame Trees will always have good memories for me because... because we've become such good friends here,' she finished weakly, not daring to claim anything more.

Jake nodded. 'I'm glad I took on the assignment in Bucharest. I'm glad we met up from time to time and renewed our acquaintance,' he said quietly. 'It's taken me a while—and a roundabout route—to get where we are at this moment, but that's better than not getting here at all.'

'And ... just where are we, Jake?' she asked, probing.

He paused. 'On a beautiful island, having a good time. Come and walk in the courtyard garden,' he suggested casually.

Despite her disappointment at his evasion, Amber smiled into his eyes and took his hand. They turned and went into the cool, airy house, their feet making no sound on the broad, polished plank floors fashioned from the breadfruit trees grown on the plantation.

'Such a lovely house ...' Amber wandered to one of the elegant rosewood tables to admire the huge vase of strelitzia, red ginger and flamboyant which she'd picked the day before. And she forced herself to bring up something that had been on her mind for a couple of days. 'We can't indulge ourselves indefinitely,' she said reluctantly. 'We ought to visit Leo soon and persuade Ginny to have those tests done—'

'But not yet,' Jake broke in quickly. 'Let's have a little more time to ourselves. Once Leo knows we're here, they'll want us to visit them, have dinner ... you know how it'll be.'

She nodded, glad to put off the meeting. Much as she loved Leo, she felt uncomfortable with the cool, reserved Ginny. Having enjoyed a successful career as an international model, Ginny would always intimidate men and women with her flawless beauty and perfect grooming.

And Amber still wasn't in a hurry for anyone to intrude on their twosome, either. She wanted Jake to herself for as long as possible. All too soon they might learn the truth about her father—and it could be something she didn't want to hear.

'If we're staying on for a while, I don't mind if we rent somewhere else,' she said hesitantly, her face saying exactly the opposite. Jake raised a disbelieving eyebrow and she laughed sheepishly. 'Well, you know what I mean. Flame Trees must be ruinously expensive—'

'No, no. I know the guy who owns it,' he explained easily. 'All I pay is the wages for the staff for the time we're here. Hippolyta, the cook, and her family normally run the place. I think they like having someone to cater for.'

'Then I'd love to stay, if you're sure it's all right,' she said with unconcealed delight. 'This friend of yours isn't short of cash, is he?' Amber looked in awe at the French antiques and rattan chairs, the cream silk and muslin drapes, and the blue and white porcelain which offset the rich, centuries-old patina of the rosewood tables. 'You couldn't have chosen a better place, Jake.'

He looked pleased. 'It's agreed, then. We'll do a bit more sightseeing and loafing around before we visit Leo.'

They paused beneath a ceiling fan. She tipped back her head and let the breeze ruffle her hair. 'We've been nothing but hedonists! I do feel rather wicked and decadent. I've never spent such a long time doing nothing!'

'You needed it. You'd pushed yourself too hard.'

Her hand touched his arm. 'I feel a lot better,' she said gratefully. 'You've taken my mind off everything. I've had a marvellous time. And you know a tremendous amount about the island. I feel I've been given my own personal tour guide!'

'I've learned to pick up information quickly,' he said easily. 'I wanted you to see all the sights—like driving into the volcano and seeing the sulphur springs. And we had to investigate the Castries market—'

'And take a ride on the bus,' she said with a grin. 'That was hilarious!'

'Noisy,' he amended drily, but his smile told her that he'd enjoyed every minute, even though the minibus had been fitted with speakers which played body-stirring calypso music at full volume.

'Don't I know it? And everyone swayed in unison; those schoolchildren in their smart uniforms—how did they manage to look so clean after a day at school?— and those friendly St Lucian women who told us about Anse La Verdure Hotel... We must go there, Jake. Perhaps for dinner, after we've seen Leo? One of the women said that St Honoré's plantation is near there, didn't she? Beau Rivage, wasn't it called?'

'Yes, I believe it was. As I said, we'll go later. It's a long drive there.' His face was in shadow, the sunlight diluted where it filtered through the louvred doors and shutters. But she thought that he had tensed. 'We have a load of things to do first.'

'Oh, good!' she said happily.

They wandered from the cool of the house to the bright sunlight of the inner courtyard, a green, green jungle of orchids and fishtail palms, the air warm with the heavy perfume of frangipani, citrus fruit and jasmine. Jake drew her closer, his arm sliding around her waist. And she waited expectantly for him to say something because her antennae sensed that he was on the brink of doing so.

Each day he'd become more alive, more affectionate. The burdens which had weighed so heavily on them both seemed lighter and they'd laughed like children as they'd fooled around on the beaches and swum in the glinting blue water.

She knew that she was falling deeply in love with him. Hope and fear filled her mind in equal measures. She was sticking her neck out again and she might get hurt. But she had to take the chance.

Amber felt sure that his heartache over Caroline was easing. Soon he might realise how close they had become. They were such good companions—content to be silent in each other's company, chatting easily at other times. It was the kind of relationship that would survive for a lifetime.

She'd never felt such happiness. It shone out of her eyes, glowed in her skin, and even she knew that the woman she saw in the mirror every night and morning was made beautiful by love.

'Amber...'

'Yes, Jake?' she said demurely, trying her best to keep her voice a low murmur instead of an excited squeak.

'I thought we'd go rafting this afternoon.'

'Oh. Right.' It wasn't what she'd been expecting. Her disappointment killed any delight she might have felt. There was time, she promised herself. Plenty of time.

'You don't like the idea?' he asked in amusement before she could recover herself and make some interested comment.

'Yes, I love it!' she said, a little over-enthusiastically.

'Not white-water stuff, I hope? I don't do courageous.'

'I think you do,' he murmured. 'Anyone who tells a border guard what he can do with his regulations and marches ten children into the arms of their waiting parents is brave in my book!' He looked down at her and his dark eyes gleamed beneath the thick lashes. 'It's a lazy, drifting-down-river kind of rafting. Does that appeal?'

It did. First they changed and gathered up what they needed—which in Jake's case meant a small rucksack and what looked like a machete but what he called a cutlass. Then they walked through the overgrown plantation, beyond the old waterwheel and the abandoned sugar vats till they came to the edge of the rainforest.

'Is it safe?' she asked apprehensively. 'We don't know much about the wildlife here, Jake.'

'I know enough,' he replied confidently. 'The path's clear and often used.' He took her hand in his. 'Come on. It's only a couple of miles.' Interpreting her puzzled glance, he said, 'I know what I'm doing. If I can navigate my way through Afghanistan and Mogadishu and deal with warlords and gangsters on the way, I can cope with a bit of Caribbean rainforest.'

'I'd forgotten,' she confessed, obediently walking alongside him.

But the reminder of his ruthless tenacity made her oddly uneasy. She slipped a sideways glance at him, noting the strength in his arms, the highly tuned body in the casual bush shirt and cut-off shorts. For the last week or so Jake had behaved like any good-looking guy on holiday. Yet he wasn't ordinary at all. He'd been trained intensively for his job, both physically and mentally—to overcome all difficulties, to be detached and objective whatever the circumstances.

She frowned. As well as stamina and talent, he needed the ability to stay cool under fire and get information out to the waiting world—no matter how harrowing the situation. What kind of man could remain impartial and report both sides of a war, as Reuters correspondents had to? Was it easy for Jake calmly to ignore his own emotions and do what was necessary?

'Mahogany.' He pointed to a huge tree.

'Oh, yes,' she said absently, wrestling with the fact that Jake might seem charming on the surface but he could be as tough as a marine when necessary. She'd heard plenty of stories about his tenacity.

She tried to pay attention to his hushed identification of some of the birds they saw. Trogons. Honey-creepers. Tanagers. Amber felt her tension increase. Cautiously she walked beneath the explosion of ferns and orchids and ducked beneath the lianas which threatened to ob-literate the path, listening to Jake's murmured com-ments. And she grew puzzled by his wealth of knowledge.

'Mind the beetle.' He eased her around a six-inch clanking monster. 'It's a Hercules beetle,' he said with a grin. 'Isn't that appropriate for such a massive creature?'

'Spot on,' she agreed as brightly as she could. But she was thinking that he couldn't possibly know so much about the flora and fauna unless he'd spent some time in the Caribbean, and he would have mentioned that, she felt sure. 'Have you ever been here on an as-signment?' she asked hopefully.

'No. I tend to stick to Europe and Africa,' he replied absently.

'You know a lot about the plants and so on,' Amber observed.

He shot her a quick look and gave her a smile which didn't seem too sincere. Her heart thudded hard. What was he hiding from her?

'I am a bit of a know-all, aren't I?' he said airily. 'I'm reading through the stack of books in my room. There's a terrific selection. Volumes on trees and flowers—and James Bond's book on the birds of the West Indies. Do you know that's where Ian Fleming got the name for his 007 hero? One of the most famous fictional spies in the world turns out to originate from an ornithologist!' His laugh was more genuine and Amber decided that she'd been imagining things.

'No, I didn't know!' she said warmly, to make up for her lack of trust.

'Fleming lived in Jamaica. He filched the name from the author of the book he used to identify the birds around Golden Eye, his house.'

They began to discuss movies they'd enjoyed and Amber happily wandered hand in hand with Jake through the magical rainforest. The tree canopy rose to about a hundred feet, making the path very dark and eerily silent—apart from the creak of soaring, eighty-foot bamboo, the rustle of leaves and the sudden flap and indignant squawk of a brilliantly coloured parrot.

They paused at the foot of a waterfall which dropped sheer into a metallic-blue pool. And a short way beyond that, beneath a huge stand of flame trees in full flower, she saw a small boathouse.

'Wait there,' Jake instructed her. 'I'll get the raft out.'

'I hope you know what you're doing!' Amber muttered, eyeing the broad river doubtfully.

'Amber!' He shook his head at her reproachfully. 'Would I risk your life, and that of your child?'

'No. You wouldn't.' She smiled. 'Go ahead. I trust you.' And she waited ankle-deep in the scarlet petals of the flame flowers while Jake unlocked the door and manoeuvred the raft to the small jetty.

'Your chair awaits, milady,' he said obsequiously.

Amber laughed. It *was* a chair too, strapped to the raft, with another chair beside it. 'It looks unbelievably uncomfortable!' she said ruefully.

'Ah, but the views...the food,' he said, plucking a couple of mangoes from a tree and solemnly placing them in front of each chair. 'The wine...' He hauled a bottle from the rucksack.

'Champagne? Jake! I wondered what you had in there! You said it was something to lubricate the works!' she exclaimed in delight.

'My works. Your works,' he replied, chuckling. 'We have music too.' He drew out a small radio and fiddled with the controls. A heavy reggae beat thundered through the virgin forest and he hastily searched for another channel. 'Sorry about that. I think I've single-handedly deafened the local population of St Lucia parrots,' he sighed, frowning till a gently romantic melody emerged from the minute radio. 'That's better,' he said, placing it on the raft. 'Maybe the parrots will be enchanted by "The Flower Song" and forgive me,' he added hopefully.

'Not if you've deafened them. They wouldn't hear it,' she pointed out.

'Get on the raft,' he sighed in mock exasperation.

'I'm getting, I'm getting! Oh! Jake!' she squealed. 'It's rocking!'

'I'm coming... It needs the two of us...to balance it...There!' he said in satisfaction, perched beside her. 'How's that?'

'Fine,' she said in amusement. 'But...who casts off?'

'Ah.' He grinned. 'Hold on. We can't sink...'

'Help!' Amber screamed as Jake scrambled for the rope and water washed over her ankles. She hung onto the edge of the chair and giggled as Jake laboriously worked his way back to his seat.

'Safe as houses,' he announced. Then he went still as he gazed at her laughing face. 'Amber!' he sighed. 'You're *edible.*'

To her joy, his mouth descended on hers. But only for a briefly sweet moment. He lifted his head blearily and gave her a long, lingering look which trapped the air in her lungs and filled her head with dreams.

'I'll be arrested for driving a raft while intoxicated,' he murmured, to her delight. 'I think I'd better stick to mangoes,' he added wryly, pushing off from the bank.

And then they were moving, drifting into the lazy current while she struggled to return to the real world again.

In a heightened state of awareness, she leaned back in the chair, conscious of Jake's arm along the back of her seat. She dared not look at his profile because she knew that her heart would lurch and she'd betray herself somehow. But every detail of his face was engraved in her mind, anyway.

For a long time they drifted along till she felt compelled to break the tense silence. 'I like rafting,' she said brightly.

'Ye-e-s. However, it does rock rather a lot whenever we lift an eyelash. We can't move about as much as I'd hoped,' he said with regret.

'Why, Jake Cavendish!' she cried in reproof. Her mouth twitched at his sorrowful glance. 'What *were* you thinking of?'

'Oh, this and that,' he said airily.

'Such as?'

'Talking.'

'You need to move for that?' she teased.

He grinned. 'I gesture a lot.'

Liar, she thought in glee. 'So talk. I'm listening.'

Her heart missed a beat as her imagination raced ahead and suggested a few things he might want to say to her. Her smile made her eyes sparkle like the glinting droplets which showered from the long sculling oar which Jake used occasionally to correct their direction.

'We need to get in the mood first,' he murmured. 'Sweet music and so on.'

'You'll have to make do with the "so on". The radio got swamped!' she said with a shaky little laugh.

'Curses! I could sing,' he offered, breaking into a husky rendition of 'Magic Moments'.

She sang too. They drifted along, singing all the songs they could think of. When the sky began to fill with soft pink, Jake smoothed cream on her exposed skin to keep the insects at bay. His hands smoothed up the line of her throat and paused as he looked deep into her eyes. And she felt herself drowning.

'I'm happier with you than I ever imagined I could be. Our marriage will work out well, won't it?' he asked appealingly.

'Yes, Jake!' she breathed, transfixed by his tender expression. Instinct prompted her to fling her arms up in the air and shout for joy. Caution kept her more composed. 'I—I enjoy being with you,' she said shyly, taking his hand. 'I'm sure we can be happy together.'

Jake kissed her soft, receptive mouth then carefully bent down and reached for the champagne. The bottle had been remorselessly shaken in Jake's rucksack during the walk, and when he eased out the cork it popped out with a loud explosion. Amber gasped as champagne drenched them both, and they ended up laughing when Jake discovered that there was only a little left to pour into the sturdy mugs.

'Never mind. I shouldn't have more than a sip. It's the thought,' she said in a kindly tone.

'Here's to thoughts,' he said huskily, chinking his mug against hers. 'Not the most elegant way to drink to our health, but... To you, Amber. To us, our future, to our child.'

'All of that,' she said, deeply happy. 'And to you. May your dreams come true.'

'Amen to that,' he breathed.

And she wondered what his dreams were—and where she figured in them.

But her frown was dispelled when Jake put his arm around her shoulders and cuddled her up to him. Dreamily they watched the sun set in the total silence of the blood-red river. Amber sighed with the beauty of it all. One by one, little pinpricks of light spangled the black sky as the raft floated towards the flickering hurricane lamps illuminating the jetty at Flame Trees.

Beneath them the river was liquid black silk now, gently pushing them towards the shore. The day was over. Overcome with emotion, Amber turned and flung her arms around Jake's neck, kissing his cheek with a vehemence that surprised them both.

'Thank you,' she said huskily. 'Thank you for a memorable afternoon.'

'Pleasure,' he said.

She felt sure that his eyes had darkened with hunger. She let her lashes flirt a little, in encouragement. But he tensed and gently eased away from her. A feeling of rejection slashed through her body like a knife.

It seemed that he ventured a little way with his emotions and then withdrew. Well, he had warned her.

Amber sat stiff and tense as he tied the raft up and stepped onto the jetty, his expression quite brittle. And his hands shook as if he didn't have complete control of them.

'Here,' he said tautly, holding out his hand to her.

'Thank you, Jake.' Deliberately, to test her theory, she half stumbled against him as she jumped from the raft. There was an immediate softening of his thinned mouth, a flicker of heat in his eyes. And then he politely stepped back.

Everything told her that he wanted to let his heart go. Something was stopping him. Caroline? she wondered.

Soberly they strolled up to the house along the lamplit path. And when she reached her room she shut the door and sat quietly, hoping with all her heart that Jake would release himself from Caroline and risk giving his love to her, because she wanted that more and more with every passing day.

Neither of them spoke much during the meal that night. Jake had asked for it to be served on the veranda and someone had dropped the mosquito nets so that they hung like a gauzy curtain between them and the tropical garden outside. Tree frogs and cicadas croaked and whirred in a jungle chorus, filling the night with exotic sounds and mystery.

'Not hungry?' murmured Jake, catching her hand and gazing at her with his dark, steady eyes.

She let her lashes drop. All through dinner she'd kept her head lowered in case he read what was going on in her mind. He was as tense and edgy as she was, both of them pushing food around their plates while the atmosphere between them thickened and pulled them closer and closer as if they were being bound together by ropes.

'No,' she managed to mutter. Her stomach was churning with nerves.

'I should take better care of you,' he said softly. 'You must be tired. Come and sit somewhere more comfortable. We'll curl up and listen to some music.' He stood up and held out his hand.

His tenderness was driving her insane. She wanted to touch him all the time, to look at him and nothing else. He kept staring at her as if mesmerised—or intent on mesmerising—and she found it hard not to meet his eyes and let him see the well of love in them. But that would frighten him off.

Slowly she stood up. Her eyes closed as a sudden spasm wrenched at her stomach. 'Oh, no!' she groaned in dismay. Her horrified eyes flew to his. The sickness! The wretched, unromantic sickness had come just at the wrong moment... 'Jake...excuse me!' She fled.

Jake kept close behind her. 'Amber! What's the matter? Do you feel ill?' he demanded in alarm.

In an attempt to keep him at bay she flapped her hand behind her impatiently. 'Mmm!'

Terribly sick. She dreaded not even getting to the bathroom in time. For the last few days she'd only had small twinges of nausea and she'd hoped that it was all over. But this was awful!

In despair, she hiked up her long, flirty skirt which she'd bought with some money that Stuart had given her and ran blindly for the bathroom.

After a while, when she was sluicing her face with cold water, he knocked politely on the door. 'Do you need anything, Amber?'

You, she thought, surprising herself. To take her mind off her feelings, she scrubbed crossly at her face with one of the fluffy white towels.

'I'm OK. I'll take a shower, Jake.'

'Of course. Want any help?'

'No!' She thought she heard a faint chuckle.

'Give me a shout if you feel ill. Promise!'

Amber promised and turned on the shower. The water slid over her in a soothing stream, helping her ice-cold body to warm up.

When she'd finished and begun slowly to dry herself, she mused on the fact that she'd conveniently forgotten all about the complication that her pregnancy presented. She was carrying another man's baby. And soon her belly would swell and Jake would find her horribly unattractive.

The bathroom door flew open and she jumped, nervously wrapping the towels tightly around her.

'Sorry to intrude, Amber, but I was worried. You'd turned off the shower. You were taking so long...' A soft light came into his eyes when she continued to stare at him blankly. 'You look all in. Come on,' he coaxed.

And before she could protest he'd picked her up and carried her to her room. She let him lay her on the big four-poster and light the lamps by the bed. Keeping his eyes rigidly on her face, he gently wrapped her hair in a towel and began to rub her body dry.

She couldn't tell what he was thinking as he reached her breasts, knew only that he was very gentle. And she noticed that he left her thighs till last, giving them only a cursory drying before tucking her up in the cool linen sheets. A small tremor of his jaw alerted her to the fact that he wasn't as unaffected as he pretended. But that wasn't surprising. He was a pretty red-blooded man and she was a woman.

Sex wasn't the problem. If she'd wanted only that, she might have had a chance. They could have agreed to relieve their physical needs together for a while. Amber heaved a hopeless sigh. She wanted far more than sex.

Her enormous eyes were very dark in her wan face. Slowly she lifted her lashes and looked up at him. 'Thank you,' she whispered, cringing with embarrassment.

He helped her to sit up against the soft pillows and dried her hair, drawing his fingers sensually through the fiery strands. And afterwards he sat close to her, staring into her eyes as if trying to discover something there.

'I'll stay with you till you fall asleep—'

'No. No need,' she jerked out. 'You've done more than enough.' With an effort she made the corners of her mouth lift into a pure apology for a smile. 'I'm afraid you've taken on more than you bargained for!'

'No,' he said, a husky tremor in his voice. 'I've dealt with sickness before. I know what it's like when a woman is pregnant.'

'Caroline,' she hazarded, pained by his wistful expression.

'That's right. She was sick for the first few months of her pregnancy, like you,' he said gravely.

'And . . . the child?'

Gentle though her query had been, it had a dramatic effect on Jake. Anguish pinched his face and he said in a strained voice, 'He died.'

He was hurting—and so was she. Amber's eyes filled with tears and she averted her head. The love in his face when he'd spoken of Caroline and her dead child was too sweet to bear. The tears rolled silently down her cheeks and she felt Jake's weight lifting from the bed, and dimly she was aware that he'd snuffed out the lamps, leaving them both in darkness. Soon he'd be gone and she could howl as much as she liked.

But in the misty, muffled background she could hear the sound of shoes dropping to the floor and then he was lying beside her—outside the sheets—but drawing her stiff, unloved body into him till they lay like two spoons together. He did nothing other than hold her. And she didn't complain because she needed him so much.

It was a while before her tears ceased. They lay together in silence and she wondered why he stayed. Pity? In memory of Caroline again? she thought a little sorrowfully.

Gradually he relaxed. His breathing became deeper and she realised that he was falling asleep. For a moment she felt angry that he could sleep so easily. After a while she turned in his arms and touched his sleeping face gently, with love. She longed for him. And always would.

* * *

At dawn, she woke and secretly luxuriated in the delight of seeing Jake's sleeping face beside her. It was like being properly married at last. His lashes lay firmly on his sabre-like cheekbones, his black curls appealingly tousled on the broad poet's forehead. He was beautiful.

When he opened his eyes she smiled and he sleepily drew her head down, his mouth so inviting that she couldn't resist. 'Mmm,' he murmured drowsily. 'Luscious. More.'

And more, and more and more... His kisses became less tender, more demanding, and Amber responded with desperate need, matching his passion with her own. Roughly he whispered to her, sweet, husky words, exclaiming over the sweetness of her mouth, the silk of her skin, the firmness of her body.

Slowly, painfully slow, his lips tracked a path to her breasts. She could hardly breathe for wanting him.

'Jake,' she sighed as his mouth explored the valley between her breasts.

He shook his head as if only now was he fully awake. In a flash he'd rolled away from her and was sitting on the edge of the bed, drawing a shaking hand across his face. 'Unfair, Amber,' he said harshly.

Amber blushed scarlet, then daringly ventured, 'Why?' very quietly. 'Because of your feelings for Caroline?'

In a quick, impatient movement, he stood up, his fists tightly clenched. 'In a way.'

She winced.

'Oh, *hell*!' he muttered, striding quickly to the door, where he paused and said gruffly over his shoulder, 'I don't want to hurt you. I have no intention of touching you again while you're still vulnerable.'

'I'm not,' she protested.

'I disagree. In any case, you will be.'

Her eyes rounded. 'What do you mean?'

Letting out a hiss of angry breath, Jake grasped the doorhandle and gave it a savage jerk. Amber thought that he seemed more annoyed with himself than her. Perhaps he was referring to the fact that Vincente St Honoré might be her father.

'I think we ought to spend today apart from one another,' Jake said quietly. 'We seem to be getting a little intense. I could do with some freedom. OK?'

It wasn't, but she could see that his mind was set on being alone. A well of misery opened up inside her. 'I want to stay here today,' she said forlornly.

'Then I'll go for a drive,' he replied. 'Anything you want me to get?'

Closer, she thought wryly. 'No. I'm perfectly self-sufficient, thanks.' Another lie. She thought of the hours ahead without Jake and felt quite lost. 'There are some books in the library I'd like to read. Odd...' she mused, going off at a tangent in the hope that the atmosphere between them would ease. 'Odd how bare the shelves are, isn't it? It's as if someone's taken most of the books away.'

'Amber,' he said, ignoring her comment, 'take care of yourself. I'll be back before dark.'

She shrugged. 'Don't rush. I'll be fine.'

At breakfast—and later, during a hasty lunch—she realised that it was the first time she'd eaten alone since they'd married. And it felt wrong. She'd been so used to Jake's company, his good humour and intelligent conversation, that she hadn't realised till now that it had become an essential part of her day.

The house seemed very empty. And she was so restless that she drove herself mad. When she finally heard his car bumping along the road, she abandoned all restraint and joyously ran to meet him, her hair flying out behind her in a river of fire.

'Hello! Did you have a nice day?' she cried, skidding to a stop and trying rather unsuccessfully to look casual.

He looked very weary and cross. 'No,' he said, sounding subdued. 'I didn't.'

'Oh.' Perversely she was rather pleased. 'I had a really lazy time, lounging around and—'

'Good.' Awkwardly he eased his long legs from the car and stretched, as though he'd been driving for hours and hours. 'I'm stiff!' he grumbled. 'I'm going to have a bath. Excuse me.'

Amber stared after him open-mouthed as he made his way into the house. He'd virtually ignored her. It had taken her an hour to decide what to wear and she'd taken ages over her face. Jake hadn't even noticed. Her body tightened defensively at his indifference.

Over dinner the tension hummed between them as they made desultory conversation. Their eyes kept meeting— hers puzzled and unhappy, his veiled and wary. He was devastatingly handsome, though. Every nuance of his behaviour she noticed and stored up; the way he held his glass, the curve of his mouth when he drank, the way his eyes smiled when he spoke to Hippolyta, the cook.

Finally, when they were sitting stiffly in the drawing room and sipping coffee like two ultra-polite strangers, she snapped.

'If you're going to be like this,' she blurted out suddenly, 'we might as well not be together.'

A wary anger flashed in Jake's eyes, startling her. 'I'm not in the mood for a row, Amber. Don't play the ultimatum game with me. I've asked you to give me a little space. That's hardly grounds for a divorce.' Slamming his cup down, he rose, gave her a curt nod and said, Goodnight.

She sank miserably into the deep armchair. The honeymoon, she thought wryly, was over. 'Goodnight, Jake,' she whispered in loving sorrow.

'Hell.'

Amber leapt to her feet in dismay. 'I thought you'd gone!' she cried crossly, blushing that he should have heard her plaintive words.

Slowly his gaze crawled up her tense body. 'No,' he muttered. 'I didn't want to go today, you see. I wanted to stay. I've thought of nothing but you all day. However hard I try, I can't excise you from my mind,' he said savagely. 'I want to hold you in my arms, tear the clothes from your body, lay you on the floor and make love to you till I have eased the terrible hunger that drives me towards you—and scares the hell out of me—so that I hardly know what I'm doing. I want you more and more each day and—'

'I'm not stopping you,' she said softly, hardly able to contain herself for joy. He wanted her, after all!

'Everything else is.'

'What?' she prompted impatiently.

His chest lifted in a huge sigh. 'I don't want you reaching for me because you need comfort, as you did with Enzo,' he muttered.

'I'm not.'

'I want you to be sure—'

'I am.'

He made a sound in his throat—a groan of pain and need which touched her heart. Amber was unaware that he'd moved but she felt herself being hauled roughly against his chest . . . her chin tipped up by strong fingers, her mouth covered by a deeply intimate, erotic kiss that made her blood catch fire. Heart and pulses leapt in frantic confusion, Jake's mouth and the pressure of his hard—sensually hard—body obliterating everything.

Her soft moan was echoed by his groan. Frenetic hands were tearing at her clothes as together she and Jake sank fluidly to the floor, consumed with the need to end their terrible longing. Amber was mindless with passion as her hands explored his burning flesh and she quivered with a feminine awe at the brute strength that was latent in the toned muscles beneath his taut skin.

In wanton need she writhed against his body, her soft, liquid eyes begging him to touch her where she burned and throbbed with emptiness.

'Tell me to stop,' he muttered rawly, grazing her nipple with his teeth.

'No. I won't. I want you, Jake!' she whispered. 'Touch me. Please, please touch me!'

Their bodies quivered in anticipation. Amber tensed, waiting, needing, her eyes hazy with love. Jake looked as if he was driven by a desperate longing. She kissed his mouth till it softened and he was crushing her to his chest so that they were cleaving to one another, skin to skin, and she knew with a soaring heart that he couldn't draw back now.

'I don't want to harm you,' he rasped.

'You won't,' she said softly. 'My baby is safe now.'

His eyes closed in pain. 'No. I mean—'

'Can't you tell what I feel?' she said urgently, touching his strained face. 'Can't we just enjoy sex with one another?' Without thinking, she shifted, and he groaned as the pressure of her thighs tantalised the rigid heat of his arousal.

'Only sex . . .' he growled.

Her mouth pressed a flurry of warm kisses on his chest. She could feel the jerkiness of his breathing, the faintly frightening throb of heat against her pelvis, see desperation in his eyes.

She buried her face in his neck, smelt the erotic, aphrodisiac scent permeating his skin, and felt a wild, uncontrollable surge of emotion. This would bind them together. And he would gently, slowly grow to love her.

'Touch me,' she whispered seductively.

And he fed her starving body with his touch while she floated on a tide of passion, watching his face through half-closed eyes. Jake wanted her badly.

'I've got to stop this,' he said thickly.

'Do so if you must. This will only happen again. You know it will,' she breathed.

'Damn you!' he muttered.

Her heart lifted at his intensely emotional exasperation. She felt him shaking through the length and breadth of his body as she whimpered for the wild sweetness of his mouth, the urgent demand of his body. And suddenly Amber felt the gentle touch of his fingers where she ached most, moving with a lightness that made her eyes close in ecstasy.

'Oh, yes, yes,' she murmured as his mouth teased her breast, slid over her waist and hips, smoothed her slightly rounded stomach. Slowly the sexual excitement built inside her till her whole body vibrated with his touch. And she felt pure, molten heat in every vein being directed to the core of her body where his fingers played their brutally gentle rhythm.

It wasn't enough, though—she wanted *him*. She wriggled seductively but couldn't escape his hold. Alarmed by his intent, her lips parted in protest; she wanted him—him—not this half-loving...

Jake's mouth took hers by storm. The caress of his fingers drove her body and mind to total oblivion as the tension within her rose to screaming point, her moans harsher, quicker as she helplessly abandoned her whole self to his touch. And then came the long, shuddering spasms of elemental energy, curling up to resonate through every part of her till she felt washed with warm desire and blissfully released.

'I have to go,' he said harshly.

Then she felt his body lift from hers and in the dim mist of sexual intoxication heard the sound of clothes being gathered up, then, a little while later, a door slamming so hard that the fabric of the house shook.

CHAPTER SIX

DISTRAUGHT, Amber lay in a stupor, physically sated but emotionally bereft. Jake had cheated her of his own surrender, his own sharing. Instead, he'd put her emotions on the line—but not his. Never his. A lump formed in her throat and she covered her face in shame for a moment before she hastily dressed and ran up to her room, trying to obliterate what had happened from her mind.

This time she didn't want to face up to it or rack herself with agonised recriminations. Deliberately she busied herself with small chores. Cleansing her face. A shower. Painting her nails and waiting for them to dry. Deciding what to wear the next day and laying the clothes out on a chair in obsessively neat order.

Then she brushed her hair hard till her scalp stung and got into bed without once looking at herself in the mirror.

There was a sharp knock on the door, making her jump. She sat up and clutched her knees, staring at the locked door in alarm as if Jake might walk through the solid wood.

'Amber!'

White-faced, she hunched up and tightened her grip on her knees.

'Open this damn door or I'll break it down!' Jake ordered.

Amber groaned. This was someone else's house. She couldn't allow Jake to smash the door down. Shakily she stumbled across the room to turn the key in the heavy

lock, scurrying back to bed as he flung the door wide
and frowned at her from under beetling black brows.

'I warned you,' he said, in a quiet, tightly controlled
voice. 'I'm not an angel. I have my limits.'

'I know.'

There was a long pause. Jake's shoulders were high
with anger. For a moment she thought he'd stride over
and maybe shake her—or hold her in his arms—but it
must have been a fanciful idea of hers because he did
neither. It seemed that he was rooted to the spot, and
his expression was a perplexing mixture of exasperation
and anger and sadness.

'Do you want anything to help you sleep?' he asked
stiffly.

She stared at him in amazement but he hadn't meant
to be ironic. 'No. I won't take pills while I'm pregnant,'
she said, her mouth sulky.

'I meant hot milk or something.'

'Is this why you were going to break down the door?'
she asked tetchily. 'To offer me a nightcap?'

Jake flinched. 'I was concerned.'

'You're extraordinarily attentive.'

'And what the hell do you mean by that?' he growled.

With a spurt of anger, she looked him straight in the
eye and said irritably, 'Oh, I don't know. It's just that
you look after me like a nephew looks after his wealthy
old aunt. If you weren't rich in your own right, I'd be
suspicious. Why do you fuss over me so much, Jake?'

'I've told you. You're vulnerable—'

'And yet you hurt me,' she said quietly.

Heaving an exasperated sigh, he leaned against the
doorjamb. 'You wanted me,' he said brutally. 'I took
away that wanting. Was that so bad?'

'Yes!' she cried, white-faced. 'I wanted you to share
yourself with me. To—to make love *properly*. But you

can't give yourself, can you? You have to stay in control all the time. You're afraid of your emotions. So you...'

She bit her lip. 'I don't want to be treated like a pet who needs stroking and feeding! That's what you did, you know. You saw I needed sex and so you callously offered me relief. I *hate* that, Jake! It's—it's like a condescension, as if you're trying to placate a dog by throwing sticks!' she finished, not caring how muddled her metaphors were. He knew what she meant right enough.

'But if I hadn't...touched you,' he said tightly, 'you would have accused me of rejecting you. Wouldn't you?'

'I might have thought it,' she muttered. 'I wouldn't have bleated it to your face.'

'On the other hand,' he went on relentlessly, 'if I'd made complete love to you, you might have accused me of using you to pleasure myself. I couldn't win,' he said with a cynical curl to his mouth. 'I was on a hiding to nothing whatever I did. And now, where do we go from here?'

'We see Leo as soon as possible and then I want to go home,' she said wanly. He was right. The only thing she really wanted from him was his love. Nothing else would satisfy her. 'Later, when we can think objectively, we need to establish a few ground rules if you want the marriage to continue.' Her ashen face lifted to his, her mouth stiff with tension.

'Curse you, Amber!' He looked back at her bleakly and then turned on his heel, pulling the door shut behind him without giving her an answer.

They were unnaturally polite to one another the next day. Amber did her best to keep out of his way; he seemed intent on doing the same. But they must have both had the same idea at lunchtime and ended up

circling each other in the kitchen while they fixed sand-
wiches for themselves.

Eventually Jake strode over and turned her around,
driving her relentlessly backwards till she felt her spine
touch the wall. 'I can't go on like this,' he said grimly.
'I never could stand cold silences.'

'I don't have anything to say,' she replied woodenly.

'I think you have a lot to say. You're punishing
me—'

'I'm punishing *you*!' she cried incredulously. He
wasn't hurting. She was. 'I doubt that,' she said, her
mouth in bitter lines. 'I'm not petty-minded.'

'We're bound to have problems. Marriage is hard
enough without the barriers we've erected between us,'
he muttered. 'I regret what happened. But you must see
that I was in a dilemma. If I'd walked away, we would
both have erupted again sooner or later. You said so
yourself.'

'So now it's my fault for speaking the truth?' she cried
jerkily. 'And my fault for letting you know how I felt?
My mistake was to be honest. Yours was to deny your
feelings. We were both wound up. You as much as
me—'

'And we should have dealt with it differently,' he said
quietly.

'I should have realised you're emotionally barren,' she
snapped.

'I'm doing my best,' he said, shaming her with his
sincerity. 'It's as tough for me as it is for you. We made
a mistake. But that doesn't mean we can never speak to
one another again, does it?'

He was coaxing her, she thought resentfully. His warm,
soothing voice was making her feel unreasonable. And
the annoying thing was that he was right. 'I didn't expect
us ever to quarrel,' she said sadly. Her long brown lashes

lifted and she looked at him with disappointment in her eyes. 'I thought we'd always get on.'

'High expectations,' he said softly. 'But you're right. That's what I thought too. And we're both more upset than we should be because we feel let down by one another.'

'I let you down?' she said with a slight pout.

His finger idly touched her lips. They parted, and she had to press them firmly together in case he thought that she was responding to him.

'I hoped you'd realise why I took the action I did,' he murmured. 'It was the only thing I could think of that wouldn't leave you as frustrated as I was.'

Her lips formed the word 'oh'. His mouth lightly touched the O and then he was smiling appealingly at her. 'I think we ought to start again,' he said, his voice throbbing in his big chest. 'When we married, my greatest wish, as you know, was that we'd gradually learn to trust one another and build a strong relationship together. I know what you've gone through. It must have rocked your trust in men. I need your trust, Amber,' he confessed.

'How can I trust you when you give only a part of yourself?' she reproached him. 'The rest is hidden. You haven't even told me much about your background—'

'I'll tell you,' he said patiently. 'When I feel I can.'

'But not now.' And she wondered what was so secret that he dared not tell her. She eyed him doubtfully, ignoring his slightly strained smile.

'It'll come,' he promised. 'Give it time. I've spent all my life hiding my feelings, Amber. That goes with the job. I've come from scenes of death and destruction, wired my report and gone off to drink slivovitz in some half-bombed bar with an informant. I'm not asking for your sympathy, only your understanding. I chose a while

ago to throw my heart and soul into my work. That
meant sacrificing my own feelings, my own needs. It's
hard to break a habit.'

His argument was compelling. Jake frowned when she
made no comment.

'If I made a mistake in choosing one of a poor set of
options,' he said, 'then I'm sorry. The last thing I want
to do is to break up our relationship or to spoil it in any
way. I think we have a lot going for us.'

'Do you?' Outwardly cool, Amber felt her legs shaking
with nerves. 'I'm not sure. I don't think my judgement
is reliable, you see. Sometimes I sense that we're close,
other times you put up shutters and I can't reach you.
Frankly I find that kind of inconsistency rather difficult, Jake.'

'It's because...' For a split second, she saw what she
thought was a hopeless desire in his eyes. And then he
turned his back.

But that split second had been long enough. Amber
took a risk. 'Because you want me—or because you need
me?' she ventured.

She saw his head tip back, the lift of his ribcage.
Something in her heart sang. It was one or the other.
But which?

He turned, his eyes, his mouth sending a raw, pulsing
shaft of love through her heart as he groaned, 'Both! I
want you and I need you. I'm obsessed with you! You
must know that. But I *will not* let you think that's all I
want from you!'

'What else do you want, then?' she breathed.

'So much,' he growled, his teeth bared in a half-savage
snarl. 'It gets worse every day. I want this...'

His mouth melted on hers and she went rigid for a
while, trying to fight her own fears. But she soon found
that she was kissing him back, moaning into his mouth

till he tore himself away and leaned back, panting, against the kitchen table.

'I have to go,' he said thickly. 'I can't stay alone with you—'

'I want you to stay!' she begged, her voice shaking with anguish.

As if protecting himself, he quickly moved so that the table was between them. 'Don't say that,' he warned, his eyes a glittering, hard black. 'I want you. I want you with a violence that consumes me. That's not what I'd planned.'

'Life rarely is,' she said shakily, guiltily glorying in his torment because it meant that he really did need her and she could build on that. 'Does it matter?'

'Yes!' he snapped. 'Do you want just a sexual relationship with me? I can give you that. Any fool can give you that! And then what? A relationship built on sex alone doesn't last. I tell you, Amber,' he said fiercely, smashing the table with his fist, 'I have no intention of ever leaving you or ever allowing you to divorce me! This must be for ever. That's why I'm biding my time. I want us to—' His mouth shut like a trap.

Amber said it for him. She drew a deep breath because it was a terrible, terrible risk that she was taking and her heart was thudding like crazy—so much so that when she spoke it seemed to have leapt to her throat and she had to force the words out in a husky croak.

'You want us to fall in love?' He flinched. 'I want that, Jake,' she said huskily. 'I want that more than anything in the world.'

For a long, electrifying moment they looked at one another. Then Jake's eyes softened. He reached out across the table for her hand and kissed it. Then he gave a crooked smile. 'You're a remarkable woman,' he said softly. 'You dare to lay your heart on the railway track with an express train coming. It makes me want to pick it up and keep it from harm. One day I will. I know it. But not now. Not yet. Can we leave it at that?'

Solemnly she studied his face. He was either sincere or the most plausible liar who had ever lived. The road to his heart was as bumpy as some of the tracks at Flame Trees, but it was worth getting there—and she was on her way, she felt sure.

'You have a reason for not letting yourself make a serious commitment to me,' she said gently. 'I believe that it's connected with Caroline—'

'Don't pursue that,' he warned in a low tone. Amber despaired of his drawn look. 'Please. Forgive me for hurting you. And spend the rest of the day with me, Amber.' He smiled at her gently, instantly touching her heart. 'I've been as miserable as hell without you.'

'You have?' she cried in shy, uncertain delight, and he laughed.

'Witch!' he grumbled.

And she felt immediately relieved that their rift had been healed. Somehow the crisis had cleared the air and forced them to go deeper into their feelings for each other. It was flattering that he claimed to be obsessed with her. But she felt even more pleased that he longed for her company. She smiled to herself. Jake was beginning to admit to the existence of his feelings about her and as time went on his heart might open.

'I feel like flying,' he said, his eyes twinkling.

'I've run out of stardust,' she murmured.

'How about a helicopter? We could fly over the island this afternoon. Nearest I can get to being a bird.'

'You could hop up and down and twitter,' she suggested.

Jake laughed and hugged her. 'I don't need any of that. I'm almost flying already,' he said softly, and touched his heart. 'Here.'

'Ring the helicopter company before I clip your wings,' she said in a prim tone.

'Tweet, tweet,' he said wryly, and flapped his arms as he hopped in a ridiculous way to the hall.

Amber followed him, laughing, and waited while he made the arrangements. Oh, she was happy! she thought. Happy because the atmosphere was genial again, happy because they were friends. They mustn't become enemies.

Almost on wings herself, she persuaded Jake to join her in the kitchen where they learnt to cook red snapper Creole-style under Hippolyta's tuition. They enjoyed that so much that they launched themselves into preparing the vegetables too—baked breadfruit and fried plantains with sliced christophine.

'The helicopter will never take off,' Amber reproved Jake, seeing him helping himself to a third helping of tropical fruit salad.

He grinned. 'You're leading me into evil ways. I'll never be able to dive for cover when I'm on an assignment if I go on eating like this.'

Her face clouded. 'I don't want you to—' Just in time she saw his head jerk up and hastily altered what she was saying. 'To get fat,' she said feebly.

It lay unspoken between them. They both knew that she didn't want him to be at risk. Already she was restricting him, behaving like a traditional wife. Mind how you go. Drive carefully. Take care. She was denying him his male need for danger because she loved him.

'It's OK, Amber,' he said, his dark eyes warm with understanding. 'I have a strong sense of self-preservation. I'll keep fit. I want to live. The idea of coming back to you is very appealing.' Her gentle smile brought a soft warmth to his eloquent eyes. 'Stop looking at me like that, sweetheart,' he said lazily, 'or I'll be sweeping the table clear for action.'

She blushed. 'I'll get my stuff ready for the trip,' she said hastily.

He chuckled as she hurried out of the room, but it was an affectionate laugh, not a sinister one. 'Sweetheart', he'd said. She hugged herself and sang happily as she changed into a cool green dress and refreshed her lipstick, and they both merrily sang calypso songs as they bounced about in the Jeep to Malgretoute, where the helicopter was waiting.

'Show us the sights,' Jake said vaguely to the pilot.

'Will do... Honeymoon?' he enquired.

Jake smiled fondly at Amber and put his arm around her. 'Honeymoon,' he murmured, as if lost in her eyes.

Within a few minutes they were strapped into their seats and ready to go.

'Sure you want to sightsee?' asked the pilot with a grin.

'Oh, yes! Jake, pay attention!' scolded Amber mildly as the helicopter took off.

But she was blissfully happy. It *was* becoming like a honeymoon. Something she'd never expected. And as they swooped down the dramatic, wave-cut east coast, with its wind-bent trees and mangrove swamps, she felt as carefree as the frigate birds they disturbed.

'The Pitons!' Jake shouted in her ear, pointing to the extraordinary twin peaks, one rising sheer from the ocean.

She nodded, her face radiant with a serene joy. 'We caught a glimpse of them when we visited the sulphur springs,' she explained to the pilot. 'But they look more spectacular approached from the sea. Beau Rivage is near here, isn't it?' she mused, remembering the name of St Honoré's plantation.

'I don't think we'll be going that way,' Jake said quickly.

'I can make a detour if you like,' offered the pilot.

'Please. I'd like that,' she said eagerly, sensing that Jake was going to veto the idea. But he just frowned and tightened his mouth a little.

The helicopter turned north along the coast for a while then the pilot pointed to a small, sandy beach backed by palm trees. 'That used to be the only way in and out, when it was a thriving plantation,' he said. 'St Honoré, the owner, let it go to rack and ruin. Everyone shunned him after he burnt down his son's house.'

Amber's eyes widened in surprise. 'Burnt it down?' she exclaimed.

'Yeah. I'll show you.'

Jake shifted in his seat. 'No. Don't bother.'

'I want to see,' she insisted, alarmed by the story. If it was true, it didn't reflect too well on St Honoré. 'I ought to check this out, in case Ginny and Leo don't know. Please, Jake. Humour me?'

He shrugged but she could see by his face that he was annoyed. 'I don't see the point,' he said irritably. 'We'll be visiting Beau Rivage in a few days. We could be spending our flying time over Marigot Bay instead, which is far more interesting. Turn back!' he ordered the pilot curtly. 'Fly along the coast again—'

'Just a sec... There!' The pilot pointed out an area in the thick forest where the tall palms gave way to shorter ones, and Amber leaned forward to look. 'That's where the house burnt down.' He pointed to a few blackened trunks still standing. 'Once there was a clearing and a road but that was ten years ago. The jungle's overtaken it all.'

Appalled, Amber sat back in her seat. 'I bet his son was furious.'

'Pascal was suicidal,' the pilot corrected. 'His wife and child were in the house. They were burnt to death.'

She flinched with horror. 'That's terrible! Jake—'

'I'll show you Beau Rivage,' offered the pilot.

He circled the scene and then went on to fly over a grand colonial house with an avenue of tall palms leading up to it and gardens as colourful as those at Flame Trees.

But all she could think of was the fire and Vincente's part in it. 'Was it an accident—the fire, I mean?' she asked in agitation. 'Was St Honoré convicted of manslaughter?'

The pilot shook his head. 'Not enough evidence. Pascal lost his rag and attacked his father, so the story goes, and was sent to prison for it.'

She was appalled. Vincente's son had lost his wife, his child and his house—and on top of that he'd had to serve a prison sentence. How awful. Instinctively she turned to Jake, but he had his eyes closed in anguish and his skin was a deathly white.

'Jake!' she cried in alarm. 'Jake, my darling, what is it? Are you airsick?' He turned his head from her, as if he didn't want her to see his face. 'I think my husband's feeling ill. Can you put us down somewhere?' she asked the pilot urgently.

'There's Pascal's place up the coast—Beau Jardin—'

'*No!*' Jake ground out harshly, jerking his head around to glare at the man. Both he and Amber flinched at the lash of Jake's eyes. 'Head back over the mountains for Malgretoute where we left the Jeep. *Yes!*' he hissed, when Amber made to remonstrate. 'It'll be quicker than putting down here and driving home on those hellish roads. *Do it!*' he ordered savagely.

Without a word, the pilot obeyed, evidently shaken by Jake's outburst. As was Amber. And she watched him in concern. His muscles were bunched up as though it was taking an effort of will to keep the sickness at bay. And she sympathised with him, knowing how helpless and angry *she* always felt when nausea struck.

'I'll drive us back,' she offered when they'd landed.

'Please,' Jake said, his voice almost inaudible.

The rest of the journey was conducted in silence. Amber concentrated hard on the road, trying to avoid potholes and places where the road had been eroded by tropical rainstorms. Tense and worried, she drove up to Flame Trees with an audible exhalation of relief.

'We've arrived, Jake,' she said gently. He opened his eyes. 'Do you want to get out or sit for a moment?'

'Out.'

But he stayed where he was and she put a hesitant hand on his, alarmed to discover how tightly he was clenching his fists and how haggard he looked. He was ill.

'I'm going to call a doctor,' she told him anxiously.

'No.' His bleak eyes met hers. 'There's nothing wrong with me. Sorry the trip was cut short,' he muttered.

'Jake!' she said lovingly. 'I understand. It doesn't matter at all. What would you like to do? Go inside in the cool or sit in the fresh air under the mango tree for a while?'

'Outside,' he said stiffly.

She fetched some iced water for him then stood watching the colour seep back into his face. 'I wish I could do something for you,' she sighed.

'Hold me!' He held out his arms.

With a small cry, she took a step forward and cradled his head between her breasts. 'Poor you,' she breathed.

'I don't want you making the journey to Rivage!' he muttered.

'But..I have to talk to Ginny!'

His arms tightened about her waist. 'It's a long journey. Halfway around the island on terrible roads. It would exhaust you.'

It would be a hard drive. And Amber thought of the accident, supposedly caused by Vincente, of Pascal's wife and child burnt to death in their house, and shivered.

'To be honest, I don't think I want to meet Vincente at all,' she admitted, burrowing her face in his hair.

Her hands absently stroked the smooth nape of his neck and she felt the love welling out from her. Kissing the top of his head, she drew back a little and kissed the lines on his forehead.

The solution presented itself. 'We'll ask Leo and Ginny to come here instead.'

Despite his nod she could tell that he was still tense and very troubled. She studied his desolate face while her mind tried to crush the niggling sensation that there were more secrets in his dark, angry eyes than there should be.

He looked up at her pale face. 'Stay with me,' he said quietly.

Her fingers lovingly stroked his forehead, and on an impulse she kissed the deep cleft between his lowered black brows. 'Confide in me, Jake,' she begged. 'I know something's troubling you.'

'It's a private hell.' He stood up, brushing her hands aside, rejecting her plea with every line of his body. 'Not for you. I'll deal with it.'

Caroline's name flashed into her mind and intuitively she made a connection. 'How did Caroline die?' she asked quietly.

And she knew the answer even before he said in a slow, broken voice, 'In a fire.'

Because she loved him, Amber stemmed her own shock and went to hug him again, wrapping her arms around him in deep sympathy. For a moment he resisted and then allowed himself the comfort she wanted to give. Tears sprang into her eyes—pity for him, of course, because he'd been cruelly reminded of Caroline's death when the pilot had talked about Pascal's wife.

But there was pity for herself too. Jake had loved Caroline so deeply that it had lasted the test of time. The tragedy must have broken his heart, she thought wanly as Jake's embrace half squashed the breath from her body.

They stood locked in one another's arms for a long time. The sky turned as scarlet as the bright bougainvillea which clambered up the veranda. The jasmine oozed its heady perfume and the bird song intensified as if the birds wanted to fill the time they had left with joy before darkness set in.

'Sweet Amber.' Jake kissed her temple. 'You're a very loving person.'

Her sorrowful eyes met his. 'I can't bear you to be upset,' she said shakily.

'I'm fine. It was a shock I wasn't expecting.'

'One of those awful coincidences,' she said sadly. 'I should have been more sensitive to your mood and realised something was wrong—'

'Oh, hell, Amber!' he said ruefully. 'Will you always try to please people and never yourself?'

'I do please myself,' she said, pink with indignation. 'Like this.' And she touched his smiling mouth then stood on tiptoe and kissed it. 'See?' she said defiantly.

'You're adorable,' he murmured with a sigh. 'Shall we go in?'

Amber nodded. Arm in arm, they strolled up to the house.

That evening Jake was more attentive, more charming than ever. Several times it was on the tip of her tongue to blurt out that she loved him. But she decided to wait a little while longer.

She went to bed feeling intensely happy, even though Jake had decided to spend the next day in Castries and had refused point-blank when she'd begged to go with him. He needed some time alone, he'd said.

Hoping that he would think a little more about their relationship and see that it posed no threat to Caroline's memory, she decided that all she could do was to be patient.

Humming contentedly to herself, she wandered through the garden the next morning, exploring more deeply than before—and becoming hopelessly lost. But the sun, she decided, should be on her left and there was a path which ought to lead her back to the house. Confidently she strode along it and came to a clearing.

At the far end was a long, low building which must have been part of the sugar distillery when Flame Trees was a thriving plantation. Filled with curiosity, she wandered over and tried the door. It was securely locked so she peered in one of the windows. And her eyes opened wide in surprise.

'How odd!' she marvelled.

One corner of the building was stacked with someone's possessions: a man's clothes, luggage, boxes of documents, family photos in frames…and a large oil painting of a dark and beautiful woman with a face so sweet and affectionate that it made her smile in response. Fascinated, she walked around the old distillery till she found a window she could climb in.

'Now, who are *you*?' she murmured, intrigued, and she edged around a cabin trunk till she could see the painting properly. There was a name on the small, gilded plate and she crouched down on her haunches to read it. 'Caroline.' Amber drew in a sharp and jagged breath. 'Caroline *Cavendish*!'

Nonplussed, she sat down on the cabin trunk, her fingers working convulsively. Already the letters on the trunk itself had emblazoned themselves on her mind. 'JC'. Jake Cavendish?

For a while her mind refused to work. Quite blank with shock, she stared at the sweet-faced woman in the painting, who looked back so gently that Amber felt uncomfortable, as if she was intruding. This was Caroline. Jake had loved her to distraction. Understandably, Amber thought grudgingly.

And then the full implications began to dawn on her. 'He lived here!' she said to herself. 'He lived here with Caroline... Caroline Cavendish. They must have been... husband and wife.'

Her teeth drove into her lower lip. Jake had kept a great deal from her. He knew more about St Lucia—more, probably, about Vincente St Honoré too—than he'd revealed. Numb, she gazed around at the carefully boxed papers, pulling a few out of their files to check the name of the recipient and the address, to confirm what she already knew.

'Jake Cavendish, Flame Trees Plantation, La Belle Dauphine, St Lucia.'

The papers dropped from her limp fingers. The house they'd been staying in had been his home. Perhaps it still was. She looked around her. It must have taken someone a lot of work to move so much stuff. Why bother? All the books must be from the library. Again, why move them?

Puzzled, she reached out to the pile of books by the trunk and flipped through two or three. Jake's name was written in each one. She tipped her head back and groaned at the discovery, realising why they'd been re-moved—to ensure that she never guessed that Flame Trees was anything more than a friend's home. Friend!

Her stomach tightened with dismay. There had been other lies. Like when he'd said that he'd been reading up on the island, its interesting tourist spots, the flora and fauna. He knew about the island already because he'd lived here. Why had he lied?

Trying not to despair, Amber held on tightly to the memory of Jake's gentleness. He did care. He felt a great affection for her. Maybe he'd wanted to bring her here because it was his beloved home...and maybe he had taken pains to hide everything to do with Caroline be-cause he'd known that it would hurt her.

And yet he had deliberately deceived her. How much more of what he'd said was untrue? She hoped and prayed that there was nothing else, no sinister threat to their happiness. Quietly she sat on the trunk and forced herself to think only of the positive aspects of their re-lationship. She remembered his sincerity, their shared laughter, the trip downriver, his care of her.

All of this typified a man who wanted their marriage to succeed, not someone who was using her for his own ends. Didn't they?

Her lip quivered. There was only one way to find out.

Jake telephoned that evening as she was striding up and down the veranda, impatiently waiting for him to return.

'I've run into a fellow journalist,' he yelled over a noisy background. 'We're in a bar in Castries.'

She felt a rush of disappointment. It would be ages before he came back. 'I can hear,' she said, trying to conceal her feelings.

'It got late before we knew it. Sorry, sweetheart. I'd better not make the journey back in the dark. I'll stay here for the night.'

'Oh. All right.' She forced herself not to question him then and there. When he answered, she needed to see his face to judge whether he was telling the truth.

'We were going on that rainforest walk,' he reminded her. 'You have to be down by the river by six or the trip will leave without you. I'm not going to make it, I'm afraid.'

Although she'd been looking forward to the trip, she was far more concerned about clearing up Jake's connection with Caroline. 'It doesn't matter—' she began.

'It does!' he insisted urgently. 'You can't miss it. I'm told that particular guide only takes half a dozen people on the walk once a month. And he knows tracks which go so deep that you'll almost certainly see species you won't see anywhere else. Please go, for my sake. Tell me all about it when you come back and make me feel a heel for letting you down.'

'Jake—' She broke off, not sure how to react. Did she believe him or not? She wasn't sure.

'Go,' he ordered. 'You'll be back just as I arrive, I expect.'

'Well...' If that was so, the trip would fill in the time...

'Tell the guide you're pregnant,' he said firmly. 'Make sure he keeps an eye on you.'

Her heart warmed a little at his concern. She'd go, and face him with her discovery when she came back. 'I'll be all right. You told me he drives you deep into the forest and we only walk for two miles. I can manage that easily. I'll take the camera so you can be envious.'

'Right. I'll see you later, then,' he said fondly. 'Sleep well and have a nice day!'

But she overslept, well beyond the time to leave for the trip. And when she saw the time and groaned she realised that it was the sound of a car outside that had woken her up.

Jake! she thought.

Amber ran to the window, intending to open the louvred shutters and call out to him. Her hand stilled on the handle. She was looking through the slats at Ginny, stepping from a car—and then there was Jake, hurrying from the house to greet Ginny and showing no surprise at all at her arrival. Amber frowned. He'd expected her to be walking in the forest that morning.

Into her mind came the idea that maybe he'd arranged the whole thing; the forest walk, his supposedly unavoidable delay in Castries, the meeting with Ginny. But she couldn't understand why he wouldn't want her to be present. Or why he had made his way home during the night or the early hours of the morning.

She went pink. Ginny would think that she was a slattern, staying in bed till after nine! As usual Ginny looked ultra-poised, ultra-beautiful, ultra-groomed. In a panic, Amber shunted hangers about in the wardrobe, despairing of finding anything remotely as smart as Ginny's gorgeously cut linen dress. Simple but screaming class, Amber thought ruefully.

'What you see is what you get,' she muttered, deciding that she might as well drag on her scarlet cotton skirt and matching short-sleeved top. But she slicked on some lipstick and brushed her lashes with mascara nevertheless. With a quick ruffle of her hectically brushed hair, she grimaced at her country-girl image and padded downstairs towards the sound of voices.

Ginny and Jake were in the library and since the door was open Amber assumed that their meeting wasn't private after all. She was about to walk in when she saw that she'd buttoned her top wrongly and paused to sort it out.

'You're mistaken!' Ginny was saying passionately. 'Vincente has been misjudged—'

'Like hell he has! You must know what he did to Caroline and the baby,' snarled Jake.

Amber straightened in surprise, astonished that they were arguing. Caroline? she thought, bewildered. And she tensed.

'I'm aware that Vincente was accused of setting fire to Pascal's house and killing Caroline and little Charles,' Ginny responded hotly. 'But he wasn't there; he swore he wasn't there!'

Vincente killed Caroline? Paling, Amber silently flattened herself against the wall and listened, her heart thumping unnaturally. Jake hadn't wanted to fly over Beau Rivage. She remembered how upset he'd been and that he'd reached out to her in need. Now she knew why and her heart ached for him.

But why hadn't he told her?

'And you believe him!' Jake was saying contemptuously.

'Yes, I do! Look, I don't have to listen to this. I came because you said it was urgent, that it involved my future—'

'It does,' snapped Jake. 'You are not Vincente's daughter.'

'Huh! Is that it?' There was the sound of a chair scraping back. 'You have axes to grind. You want to cause trouble. I've heard about you, Jake,' she said tightly. 'You loathe and despise Pascal because you think he seduced Caroline and got her pregnant!'

Amber's eyes widened. It hurt her that Jake had kept so much from her. They hadn't been close at all. It had been nothing but her own desire to be part of Jake's life that had persuaded her otherwise.

'Pascal's reputation was appalling,' Jake bit out. 'Anyone in their right mind would have acted in Caroline's interests and condemned the affair—'

'They loved each other!' Ginny declared indignantly.

Jake's breath hissed in painfully. 'I know that now,' he growled. 'Someone...close to the family told me a short while ago. Do you think that makes it any easier for me?'

Amber choked back a sympathetic cry. It couldn't have been pleasant for Jake to acknowledge that his wife had loved another man. She was about to turn away when she heard Jake speak again.

'Anyway, Pascal isn't Vincente's son, is he? No wonder Vincente was frantic to find his rightful heir.' Amber could hear him striding up and down, his pace fast and heavy as if he was very angry. 'Pascal was passed off by Vincente as his own son,' he went on relentlessly, 'to hide the fact that his sister had given birth to an illegitimate child.'

There was a hushed silence. 'No one outside the family knows that!' Ginny said shakily. 'Susannah's only just told Pascal she's his mother—'

'I know. I talked to Susannah and Pascal yesterday,' snapped Jake.

Amber tensed. That was what he'd been doing! More lies, she thought miserably.

'Now, if Pascal isn't Vincente's son and you're not his long-lost daughter,' Jake went on, 'then it looks as if the whole estate will go to Susannah. I doubt Vincente would like that. There's no love lost between them, I gather.'

'But I *am* his daughter,' cried Ginny angrily.

'Then I challenge you to take the test to prove it.'

'Don't cause trouble!' warned Ginny. 'You're still waging an old vendetta, Jake—one you should have abandoned long ago. Vincente's brother-in-law has confirmed who I am. He ought to know; he sheltered Vincente's wife when she ran away! He was there at my birth; he must have known who adopted me!'

Amber could bear no more. Trembling, she went to the doorway. 'Jake!' she cried, wringing her hands.

'Amber!' he growled, whirling around. 'You're supposed to be out.'

'I know. I overslept and missed the trip.' She straightened, realising what he'd said. His remark had confirmed her fear. 'Did you arrange this meeting, Jake, knowing I'd be out?'

'Yes,' he said curtly. 'I didn't want you involved.'

Her eyes flashed. 'But I am—and I don't like being left out of something that concerns me. Ginny, you must take the test. Jake's right. What I hear of Vincente horrifies me—'

'You don't know him!' said Ginny, near to tears. 'He's not anything like as bad as he's been painted! He's dying. The stories about his treatment of his wife are inflated out of all proportion.'

'He's a monster!' muttered Jake, his eyes black with loathing.

'No. And I refuse to stay here and listen to your poisonous lies!' yelled Ginny furiously. 'OK, I'll take the test and send you the proof! And if you've got any sense,' she snapped, glaring at Amber, 'you won't let Jake involve you in his ill-conceived revenge! Examine his motives, Amber! And don't trust him an inch!'

CHAPTER SEVEN

GINNY strode out, her bobbed hair swinging vigorously. And the vehemence of the woman's outburst left Amber shaking. Ginny was always so cool and collected, utterly in control of herself.

She'd spoken of revenge. Was that all Jake wanted? Amber sat down before her legs gave way. Jake's watchful eyes rested on her unnervingly. Doubt filled her mind. Jake had a strong motive to hurt the St Honoré family. Vincente had apparently killed Caroline and her baby. Jake's baby, she thought with a wince. And they'd been in Pascal's house at the time—Pascal, the man Caroline had really loved.

'Oh, Jake!' she groaned. Was he using her as a means to exact some awful revenge?

'I must tell you about Caroline,' he began grimly.

'I know about her.' She paused while a long, slow breath was exhaled between his teeth. At the moment she felt numb with pain. 'I saw the things you'd hidden in the shed when I was out walking yesterday,' she said unhappily. 'The picture of Caroline. Your books. I—I realised that this had been your house. I knew you'd lived here. Not Kenya.'

'I never claimed I lived in Kenya.' He sat on the opposite side of the library table, his face a stony mask. 'You assumed I did because my parents are there now.' He looked down at his linked hands. 'They went to Kenya with me after the inquest on Caroline and Charles because they couldn't bear to stay.'

'Why didn't you tell me?' she flung at him. 'Were you afraid I'd be jealous?'

He looked puzzled. 'Jealous of the love I've always felt for Caroline and Charles? No, Amber, that wasn't the reason. I never believed you to be petty and possessive.' And she blushed, because of course she envied the immense love he still bore for the other woman. 'I didn't want you to know that my family had previous connections with the island.'

Very slowly her head turned towards him. What was it that Ginny had said? 'Examine his motives'. 'You pretended you wanted to clear up the doubt about Ginny being Vincente's daughter. I think you have other reasons. And that's why you've been lying to me . . .' She swallowed to clear the lump in her throat. 'Perhaps about everything,' she suggested huskily.

'You see?' he said angrily. 'Vincente has already poisoned Ginny's mind and the poison's spread to you. Now you're doubting my intentions.'

'Then tell me what they are and let me judge for myself,' she said in a choky little voice.

'I want you to have what I believe to be rightfully yours.'

Her eyes narrowed. She had a feeling that he'd left something out. 'And if it isn't?'

He shrugged. 'We will be happy together wherever we live, whatever we do, whoever you are. I don't care if you're the daughter of a gillie or a lord or—'

'If my father is Vincente,' she began carefully, 'won't that be an impossible situation, since you believe he killed your wife and child?'

'Wife?' Jake looked genuinely puzzled.

How clever he was, she thought, upset. He would have fooled the Inquisition. 'Caroline,' she reminded him scornfully.

To her contempt, his astonishment deepened. 'She wasn't my wife! What ever gave you that idea?'

'Caroline *Cavendish*,' she snapped. 'Don't play the innocent, Jake; it won't wash. Her name was on the little plate below her picture.'

'That doesn't make her my wife,' he said quietly.

His sincerity made her conviction waver. Perhaps she'd jumped to the wrong conclusion. A cousin, maybe, she thought, clutching at straws. 'I can check, you know,' she warned.

'You're welcome to. You sidestepped the most obvious connection. Caroline was my sister.'

Amber's stiffly held body slumped back into the seat. 'Your sister?' she repeated uncertainly. Her eyes flickered up accusingly. 'You told me you had no brothers or sisters...'

'I don't, thanks to Vincente St Honoré.'

She winced when she thought of Caroline's and Charles's shocking death. 'Oh, Jake!' she said softly.

'She was my older sister but in many ways she was more like a kid sister. When I was old enough I took it on myself to protect her. She was far too sweet-natured and trusting for her own good,' he said, his eyes quite desolate with memories.

Amber blushed with shame. Jake couldn't fake that look. He was telling the truth and she felt like a heel. 'I'm sorry,' she mumbled. He came to crouch down beside her and put his hand on her knee. 'Ever since you first spoke of her,' she continued, 'I thought you and she were lovers.'

He groaned. 'I wish you'd asked. It never occurred to me... Amber, I'm sorry. But... why did you jump to that conclusion?' he asked tenderly.

'The way you spoke. The way you looked when you thought of her. And when I saw her picture... She was very beautiful,' she said in a small voice, reliving her jealousy.

'Yes,' he agreed, his voice tight with strain.

'Oh, Jake, I can understand why you are so bitter about Vincente,' she said shakily. 'But I'm worried about why we're here. There's more to it than checking out the claims that Ginny or I might have to Beau Rivage. Something else is motivating you—something so powerful that you've brought me here, halfway across the world, to help you to achieve it. What is it, Jake?'

'Justice.' The word was softly spoken but with a savagery that made her shiver.

Her fears were confirmed. Aching for him, drawing her fingertips over his stark cheekbones in the hope that she could ease his pain by touch alone, she said sadly, 'When is justice another word for revenge?'

'Amber!' he said urgently. 'Do you think I can stand by when I am certain that Vincente and Ginny are living a lie? She has no right to the plantation. Other people in the St Honoré family are involved. They deserve the truth. They're relying on me—'

'Oh, yes,' she remembered. 'You met Pascal and his mother yesterday.' It was rather frightening, thinking that she might have relatives here. Strange people in a strange country. With strange habits; feuds, hatreds, dark secrets. 'What—what are they like?'

Jake squeezed her hand as if he knew what was going through her mind. 'Pascal is striking. Fair, blue eyes, athletic, tough and tanned—and extremely hostile at first, naturally. But after we'd talked for a while we got on rather well together,' he admitted. 'Partly due to his wife, Mandy.' He smiled absently. 'She's pregnant. Very open, warm and friendly. They seem very happy together.'

She envied them that. 'And Pascal's mother—Vincente's sister?'

'Susannah?' Jake's eyes narrowed thoughtfully. 'Embittered, I'd say. Fiercely protective of Pascal. She hates Vincente. Can't bring herself to say his name.'

She blanched. 'Did you . . .?' Her voice wobbled. 'Did you tell Susannah and Pascal that you think I'm his daughter?'

'I told them I am sure of it. Susannah was shocked. I got the impression that she knows that Ginny's claim will be disproved—'

'And Susannah is hoping to inherit,' finished Amber. 'Mind you, Vincente could leave everything to a friend, or a cats' home.'

'He won't do that. He represents an old French dynasty. Vincente is very proud of his ancestors and anxious about his descendants. He'll leave Beau Rivage to someone who has his blood in their veins. Preferably his own child,' he added softly.

She drew in a harsh breath. Jake meant her. It was too horrible to consider. 'How can you be so sure Vincente is my father?' she asked miserably.

His eyes were full of compassion as his fingers lightly touched the silver locket around her neck. 'Because the picture inside your locket is a photograph of Vincente's wife,' he said simply. 'Yesterday I looked at the newspaper cutting of their wedding. There is no doubt, Amber.'

Her mouth quivered. Evidence was building up. 'Then we must see Vincente and talk to him,' she said nervously.

'There's no point in seeing him—'

'But this man is possibly my father!' she cried, distraught. 'I wish he weren't. I wish Angus and Elizabeth were my parents and I'd never, ever heard of Vincente St Honoré!' she wailed, tears filling her eyes.

'Sweetheart,' he soothed, kissing her unhappy mouth, 'he won't listen to anything we say. He won't want to know. Wait till Ginny gets her test results.'

'I can't wait,' she said jerkily. 'I must see him. I can show him the locket and tell my story and see what he says. *Please*, Jake!' she begged, her eyes glistening. 'Now. Let's get it over with!' Before she changed her mind, she thought. Before she asked Jake to take her home and forget that St Honoré existed. 'Right now. This very minute!'

It was a long time before he answered, and when he did he sounded reluctant. 'OK. If that's really what you want.' Jake's sudden tension communicated itself to her. 'It'll mean driving up to Dennery, across the mountains to Anse La Raye and down the coast road,' he told her quietly. 'I think, because of your condition, we'd better take the Range Rover and break the journey overnight. We'll have a better chance of talking things through with Vincente if we're not worrying about getting back before dark.'

It wasn't until they were driving through the mountains that she understood why Jake had made that suggestion. The road wound slowly in great twists and turns up into the mountains and a few miles took an age. To make the drive more difficult, a tropical rainstorm hammered like nails on the roof of the Range Rover as if it meant to drill holes in it. The noise was deafening. Jake could hardly see a foot ahead, even though the windscreen-wipers were working like crazy.

'A hundred and sixty inches of rain a year!' he yelled.

'Today!' she corrected him ruefully.

He grimaced and leaned forward, straining to see where the road went. It seemed that water gushed down on them from all sides, pouring off the steep, forested sides of the narrow ravine and tumbling down the rough road behind them as if it might wash them away.

Strangely, it made Amber feel exhilarated. She and Jake against the elements. It was a far simpler contest than the recent battles she'd had with her emotions. He was very skilled, strong, keen-eyed, determined. A man to have on your side. She relaxed, glad that he was on hers.

'Looks worse than it is,' called Jake.

'I'd be scared if I were with anyone but you,' she admitted.

'Thanks, sweetheart! Hey! It's stopped! And look— a rainbow!'

'Two. Three—oh, Jake!' she cried in awe. 'Four rainbows! So clear...aren't they beautiful?'

'Beautiful. Let's take a break.' He drove to the side of the road and switched off the engine with a sigh of relief.

'You must be exhausted. Shall I dig out the snack that Hippolyta made for us?' she suggested.

'Sounds good. Banana bread and garlic chicken. I'll eat it if you will,' he murmured.

'The banana bread?'

He fixed her with a meaningful look. 'Garlic.'

Amber went pink. She reached down and took a bite of the chicken. He did the same. And then he put the spicy chicken leg down and leaned over, turning her head with a gentle finger on her chin.

She opened her mouth to speak, but his lips were covering hers and for the life of her she couldn't remember what she'd meant to say. It was a gentle kiss, but intensely erotic, and as her bones began to soften his body came up against hers, hard and demanding.

Amber was clinging to him, blindly grasping at his shoulders, her mouth moving with his in a desperate attempt to crush all her fears. She had been scared; she acknowledged that. And the journey itself was something of a nightmare. Her courage had made her demand the meeting but she was dreading it. And in his arms she felt a warm sensation, felt safe and happy, protected from all harm.

'Amber,' he said roughly. 'Amber, Amber!'

He pulled her across him so that she straddled his thighs. She felt the touch of his hands on her bare legs, smoothing her calf muscles, her shins, sliding up the silky skin, unbuttoning her top.

'We should stop. You said...' Her protest was muffled by his mouth, which obliterated everything in her head.

'I love you,' he said in her ear.

She froze. Her startled eyes met his and then he was kissing her again—her mouth, throat, her shoulder... breast. 'Jake!' she whispered. 'What did you—? Jake—?'

'I love you,' he said, his eyes blazing up at her. 'I love you. Here,' he growled, gently taking her hard nipple in his warm mouth. 'And here...' He kissed her fast-beating heart and it lurched uncontrollably. 'Feel my heart,' he ordered. 'Feel it!'

He pushed her back a little. Holding her breath, she reached out and placed her hand on his chest. His heart leapt as if it were a living creature. 'This isn't just...sex?' she whispered.

'Oh, yes, that too,' he admitted, his eyes dancing wickedly. 'I want everything. I've wanted that since I first met you. But it was obvious that you were a woman of deep emotions and I felt that it would be unfair to ask you to share my life—'

'Why?' she demanded.

'I told you. Reporting wars isn't exactly wife-friendly,' he said wryly. 'I did my best not to get involved because I knew I could fall for you in a big way.' He smiled and fondled her hair. 'Every time I weakened I thought of us being married and how I'd go off on an assignment, worrying about you and whether you were worrying about me. I knew I'd be in a hell of a mess!'

Amber took his face in her hands and kissed him tenderly. 'You idiot!' she sighed. And thought of Enzo. She winced. 'If only—'

'Never mind,' he murmured, stroking her hair and looking deeply into her eyes. 'Forget the past. We're together. We'll work out a way of living the kind of life we can both accept. I want you to be happy, Amber.'

'I am,' she said fervently. 'I am, Jake!'

'Kiss me, sweetheart,' he crooned, his voice as soft as butter. 'Kiss me.'

She was boneless, all mouth and limbs. And he... Her hands explored him, feverishly pulling at his shirt buttons, pushing up the shirt when she became impatient, the pads of her fingers pressing against his chest. Her head tipped back, the mass of her fiery hair caressing her naked back, her hunger for him ungovernable.

They were married. They loved one another. She could deny him nothing. And when his tongue darted out to taste her erect nipples she gasped, shaken by the strength of her feelings. It was more than sex, she thought hazily; more than a primitive need. It was a sharing.

'Jake,' she moaned, her voice harsh and unreal in her ears. She arched against him, an untaught, voluptuous siren, and he responded with a kiss so deep and passionate that she rocked with its intensity.

He held her head in his hard, masterful hands. 'Love me!' he husked, his body taut with anguish.

'My darling,' she sighed. 'I do love you...'

Endearments whispered from his fevered lips. He caressed her with great skill, driving her into a tempestuous state of longing that held her on a thin thread of consciousness, only part of her aware of what she was doing and the rest—the rest was all miraculous sensation, wanton, erotic, uncontrollable.

Vaguely she was aware that she was colluding with their sensuous slither into the back seats, her smooth skin brushing now against his naked body. She felt the hard maleness of him, inhaled the intoxicating scent of his warm face and surrendered everything to him.

His mouth explored the smooth contours of her body while his hands tormented each breast till she couldn't bear the agonising sweetness.

Jake groaned, kissed her, whispered that he loved her, touched her face in wonder and gently lifted her hips. She felt the hard heat of him, the strong, cautious movement inside her body, and she shuddered long and low.

'You...you want me to stop?' Jake's words sounded slurred.

'No, my darling,' she moaned raggedly. 'I'm not hurting. I'm h-happy!'

'I worship you,' he whispered against her mouth.

And gently they moved together—a sweet gentleness that captured the deepest core of her heart as she gazed into his loving eyes until the darkness of passion forced her lids to close and her body pulsed with unbearable demands.

The world outside receded until it contained only them. She and Jake, the fire of his body, the supple receptiveness of hers. Nature had taken over. Their movements were perfect, in glorious unison, giving their bodies a fierce urgency that was echoed in their hearts.

Their breathing became harsher. Sweat slicked between them, easing the slide of their bodies. Amber cried out her love and Jake muttered something, far in the distance of her mind, as every part of her soared to reach the crescendo and slowly, beautifully eased every muscle in her body and his.

They lay supine. She couldn't speak for happiness. His heart was crashing alarmingly against his ribs and she listened as it gradually became calmer and all the while he hugged her as if she'd vanish if he stopped.

Tenderly he shifted his position and tucked her up in his arms. 'Sleep for a while,' he murmured softly, kissing her still closed lids.

She heaved a contented sigh, washed in love. There had been a tremor in his voice that tore at her heart. He loved her. They would be blissfully happy.

That night, when they stopped at a small hotel in Anse La Raye, he held her lovingly and stroked her naked body as if he wanted to emblazon every inch on his mind.

'Yes,' he said shakily, when she invited him with her eyes. 'I want to. I can hardly hide that,' he said ruefully. 'But I don't want to tire you and it'll be a tough day tomorrow, I think.'

She blotted out tomorrow. Tomorrow was tomorrow. This was today and Jake loved her. 'I—' She blushed. 'I can... I can make love to you,' she said timidly.

'I don't—'

But she touched him. And his eyes closed in deep pleasure. That night she learnt more about love. She became bold and eager to learn because she wanted to please Jake more than anything in the world. And in the morning she still swam with the pleasure he'd given her because it had been given with love too.

Beau Rivage turned out to be more run-down than it had looked from the air. Obviously Leo had begun to put in a lot of work on it, but the once grand house was still suffering from years of neglect and builders seemed to be swarming everywhere.

It was a sun-faded house of traditional woods, filled with beautifully cared for French antiques. She and Jake waited in the silent hall, wondering if Vincente would agree to see them. Neither Ginny nor Leo seemed to be around and Amber was a little relieved. She didn't want Leo to think that she was taking sides against his wife.

Jake had gone very quiet. When she glanced anxiously up at him, she saw that his face looked almost grey and his eyes burned very brightly and were as hard as coals. His stillness was the uneasy calm of a hurricane's eye.

'I'm scared,' she said breathily, worrying about Jake's hatred for Vincente. And for once he didn't reassure her. It seemed that he was lost in a world of his own. Amber gulped, an icy chill settling on her spine.

'Monsieur St Honoré will not see you,' announced the young St Lucian woman who'd opened the door to them and who'd introduced herself as Jemima. She looked embarrassed and apologetic.

'He has to,' retorted Jake shortly.

'No, he don't, Mr Cavendish,' said Jemima in her musical voice. 'He's a sick man. He sees who he chooses and you didn't make an appointment.'

'Tell him,' Jake said tightly, 'that it concerns Mary and Castlestowe.'

The maid shrugged and wandered into the depths of the house. Amber felt goose-bumps all over her skin and moved from beneath the lazily turning paddle-fan. And the maid returned before she had plucked up the courage to ask Jake what difference those names would make.

'Monsieur St Honoré will see you in the garden. Straight through the house, out the back door,' reported Jemima, her eyes big and startled.

Jake grabbed Amber's hand. 'Come on,' he said grimly.

'Mr Cavendish . . .'

Impatiently Jake looked back at the worried-looking maid. 'What?'

Amber stiffened. That wasn't like Jake at all. Or...was it?

'It's none of my business what you do here,' said Jemima politely, 'but he's dying, Mr Cavendish. You remember that and go easy.'

In his present, odd mood, Amber expected Jake to make some brief acknowledgement—a mutter, perhaps— and stride on. To her surprise, he frowned at the maid and considered her thoughtfully.

'You're very loyal,' he said, almost as a challenge.

'He had a bad time,' said Jemima defiantly. 'People say he's wicked. Miss Ginny and Mr Leo know he's not. It's all gossip and no facts.'

'Really?' Jake didn't sound convinced. 'Perhaps we could have a talk later, Jemima. You can tell me why I should believe you.' And then he hurried Amber through the house, his hand painfully gripping hers.

In the garden below the veranda was a man sitting beneath a silk-cotton tree. His legs were covered in a blanket but Amber could see how thin and frail he was. His hair was grey and wispy and he was coughing into a handkerchief. Despite her mixed feelings she felt sorry for him. He did look very ill.

Instinctively she turned to Jake. 'Don't hurt him,' she said softly.

'I can hardly avoid that.'

Her hand stroked Jake's arm, coaxing him to have some compassion for Vincente. 'He could be my father,' she reminded him.

'That doesn't automatically make him worthy of your affection or your respect,' Jake said quietly.

And before she could remonstrate with him he caught her elbow, leading her down the steps to the garden. With an obvious effort Vincente lifted his head at the sound of Jake's approaching stride and eyed them as they came to a halt in front of him.

'I am Jake Cavendish. This is my wife.' Jake's abrupt introduction showed no pity for the sick man.

Vincente studied them both with watery brown eyes. Amber noticed that the hands which clutched the blanket were shaking. 'Cavendish of Flame Trees?'

Jake gave a curt nod. 'Caroline's brother,' he said in a lacerating tone, as if intent on driving the fact home.

It seemed that the old man didn't expect politeness because he showed no surprise at Jake's abrupt manner. 'Ginny warned me you were back. You mentioned something about... Mary? And Castlestowe?' he asked hoarsely.

Jake pulled up a chair for Amber and waited till she was seated. 'You know Ginny isn't your daughter,' he stated without preamble.

'Like hell I do!' Vincente protested. 'Stuart is certain of it.'

Amber stiffened warily. 'Stuart?'

'My brother-in-law,' explained Vincente irritably, and Amber relaxed her tensed muscles. 'He looked after my wife, Mary, when she left me. He knows that Ginny's my daughter. He rang from Castlestowe some time ago and assured me—'

Amber heard no more of Vincente's explanation. Castlestowe, she thought, her body suddenly turned to stone. 'Stuart?' she said incredulously. 'Do you mean...Stuart Brandon?'

'Yes. My wife's brother.' Vincente took a sip of water and leaned back in the chair, watching curiously as a range of emotions flooded over Amber's face. 'Didn't you know? My wife was Lady Mary Brandon.'

She flung Jake a questioning look but he was totally intent on Vincente, the hatred pouring out of him as though he would have dearly loved to take the old man by the throat and throttle him then and there. Amber quailed.

'Stuart doesn't have a sister!' she exclaimed.

'To all intents and purposes,' Jake said quietly, 'that's been true for the last twenty-five years.'

'Nobody even mentioned her name...' she began.

'You told me yourself how Castlestowe is the kind of community that protects its own members. The old Earl and Stuart were deeply shocked when Lady Mary vanished. There was an unspoken agreement that her name would never come up in conversation again. And Stuart removed all her pictures to save his father any more distress.'

Slowly she absorbed this information, dismayed to find that she was on shaky ground again. 'You knew that it was Stuart who'd cared for Vincente's wife when she ran away...and Stuart who had backed up Ginny's claim!' Her eyes darkened in accusation and reproach.

'Of course. I couldn't tell you,' he said stiffly. 'If you'd known, you'd never have agreed to challenge it.'

Confused, she touched the locket around her neck. 'Jake,' she said, trembling, 'Stuart has no reason to lie—'

'Oh, but he has.' With an impassioned gesture, Jake caught her hand in his. 'If he tells the truth, he could lose you. And he wants to keep you with him more than anything in the world.'

'But Leo is his son!' she cried impatiently. 'By saying that Ginny is Vincente's daughter, he has lost Leo, the heir to his estate! It doesn't make sense, Jake!'

'It does,' he said fiercely. 'We've talked of this before. Remember?'

'At our wedding,' she answered reluctantly.

'Listen. Stuart had a choice. To lose Leo or to lose you. We both know he's closer to you than to his son. He has seen you grow up. You love him and he loves you. You are the daughter he never had—'

'Leo is his *heir*!' she protested.

'And as his son and heir Leo had a different treatment—including a strict discipline that didn't leave much room for love. But Stuart could indulge you and you reached his hidden heart. He had a choice—a hard one. Love or duty. He chose love. You. And by keeping you with him he can leave Castlestowe to you—'

'To me?' she said, bewildered. 'But why would he do that?'

'Haven't you grasped it yet? You have Brandon blood. You're his sister's daughter. You are the daughter of Lady Mary Brandon.' He had reached around to the back of her neck and was fiddling with the clasp on the chain that held her locket.

She jerked her hand up to stop him from removing it but was too late. 'No, Jake, no!' she wailed as he held it out to Vincente.

'You were advertising for Amber Elliott,' Jake said to the pale-faced old man. 'This is Amber. And this, I believe, is your wife with Amber shortly after her birth.'

Amber trembled, her eyes huge with anticipation. Vincente would open the locket. He'd say, No, this isn't my wife. She and Jake would walk away and... Oh, open it, open it! she begged silently and impatiently as Vincente's nicotine-stained fingers fumbled with the delicate fastening. Hardly breathing, her heart seemingly in her throat, she waited and waited for the verdict.

Everything was riding on this: Ginny's future, Leo's, Stuart's. Hers. Jake's.

The locket snapped open and Vincente stared at it for a moment then shut it up again. He leaned back in the chair, closing his eyes.

'Amber is your child,' said Jake softly, with a terrible conviction. 'And she is my wife.'

'A Cavendish,' muttered the old man with distaste. He looked up suddenly, his hands shaking more visibly. 'Do you... do you have children?' he growled.

There was a challenging lift to Jake's chin. 'My wife is pregnant. Your grandchild will be a Cavendish, and a Cavendish will own Beau Rivage when you are gone.'

He let that sink in for a moment. 'Poetic justice, I think,' he said softly.

Vincente gave a little moan. Amber couldn't move. She was paralysed with shock. Jake's motives were suddenly horrifyingly suspect. He'd extracted a promise from her that no one should know that he wasn't the father of her child for at least ten years. That meant that Vincente would go to his grave believing that Jake's child stood to inherit the estate. It would be a fitting revenge.

Her child was a crucial factor in Jake's plan. It wasn't surprising that Jake was concerned for her welfare. It was as if he'd been nurturing a valuable brood mare, she thought angrily.

She and her unborn baby were a package. Maybe Jake was genuinely quite fond of her. Maybe he also found her sexually attractive. But his overriding need had been to draw her into his web and make her fall in love with him till she hardly knew or cared what he was doing.

Bitterness twisted her mouth. 'I don't look like Lady Mary. I don't look like Vincente. That isn't your wife, is it?' she cried, willing Vincente to nail the lie.

'Amber, do you remember the portrait of Stuart's mother and how closely you resemble her?' asked Jake, when Vincente remained silent. 'The old Earl saw the similarity—so did you. You've inherited the Scottish colouring of the Brandons. You've always had a special bond with Stuart—and he with you. Now you know why. He's your uncle. This is why he cared for you so much and treated you like one of the family—because you *are* part of his family—'

'No!' she cried, covering her ears. 'No, no, Jake!'

Jake gently pulled her hands away. 'You must listen,' he insisted.

'My mother's Dorothy Elliott...' she began stubbornly.

'No, Amber. We're dealing with a massive cover-up here. Let me explain.' Jake sat on a wicker chair beside her, his eyes anxious and loving.

Amber tried not to be swayed by her emotions. She had to weigh up the facts as objectively as possible. 'Well?'

'After caring for his sister for a few months, Stuart booked her into the nursing home near Glasgow because it offered more anonymity than the nearer ones in Oban,' he explained. 'Before the birth Mary stayed in a small flat near the nursing home because she had to go for check-ups and travelling was an ordeal for her.' He flicked a glance at Vincente. 'You know why.'

The older man shifted in his chair. 'My wife was terrified of open spaces,' he muttered reluctantly. 'Agoraphobia.'

'You can imagine,' Jake went on, 'how desperate Mary must have been to leave her husband, if she opted to travel from St Lucia to England.' The words hung in the warm, flower-scented air, condemning Vincente. 'Well, the short distance from the flat to the nursing home was still something of a nightmare for Mary. She arrived for her first check-up at the nursing home in something of a state. Two women calmed her down and befriended her. One was Sarah Temple—'

'Ginny's mother,' she remembered, thinking of the newspaper cuttings.

'That's right. The other woman was Dorothy Elliott. Both Dorothy and Mary were anxious not to be traced by their husbands. Dorothy was sporting a black eye and bruises from her feckless husband's most recent battering. When Dorothy said she'd give anything to escape her marriage, Mary saw her chance. The two women exchanged identities there and then, before they registered. And Dorothy went to live in the flat with Mary till their confinements.'

Amber swallowed. It was a good story. But Jake was a journalist and a good writer. Fiction wasn't beyond him. She flashed a quick glance at Vincente. He was leaning forward as if he'd been hanging on Jake's every word.

'Presumably I can check this with Stuart,' she said unevenly.

'You can. He knew Mary had befriended the two women and he was glad she had support from Dot and Sarah... Something wrong, Amber?' he asked gently.

Frowning, she said, 'It's the names. They seem familiar... Never mind. It'll come to me. Go on. What happened then?'

'Sarah remained with her child and eventually took her away. Dot and Mary vanished, leaving their babies in the home,' he said gravely.

'They went away together?'

'Mary couldn't have made it without Dot,' answered Jake quietly.

And he seemed to be watching her, as if prompting some part of her memory, waiting for something to fall into place. But her mind was in too much of a turmoil to make any clever connections.

'Why did they abandon their babies then disappear?' Amber asked sadly. 'They had somewhere to stay—'

'You forget.' Jake gave Vincente a malevolent glance. 'Mary preferred to vanish rather than risk Vincente tracing her through Stuart. She left soon after Stuart had taken the picture—the one in your locket, Amber.'

'And Dorothy?'

'She was very scared of her husband too. She felt her child would be safer with adoptive parents than with her.

And Stuart asked Elizabeth and Angus Fraser to adopt you. He wanted to have you near, you see.'

'Very glib,' muttered Vincente.

'Very true,' countered Jake, his jaw jutting out in challenge.

Amber tried to get up but sank in a heap on the ground, her legs having given out. This man might be her father and Jake loathed him. Where did that leave her? She fixed her huge eyes on Vincente. 'Tell me that isn't my mother's picture in the locket!' she pleaded softly.

Vincente's eyes filled with tears. His shaking hand reached out and touched the rich fire of her hair. 'It is. You know it is. Oh, my child!' he said brokenly.

And she cried. Her head drooped to rest on Vincente's lap while she sobbed her heart out. In the background she could hear Jake's tight, angry growl as he spoke to Vincente, but she was only thinking of herself now. Somehow she would have to adjust to being the daughter of this notorious rogue...

'Don't cry,' said Vincente thinly. 'I don't blame you for thinking I'm wicked. Your husband has poisoned your mind.'

'No,' she denied, not wanting that to be true. 'He's interested in justice. He only wanted to help me find my real parents—'

'I doubt that.' Vincente tried to stop her from jumping up in distress but she evaded his hand and drew back, her eyes wide with apprehension. 'I'm sorry, Amber. You'll learn what Jake Cavendish wants, why he's gone to all this trouble to dig up information...which begs the question,' Vincente growled, 'of how he has learnt...all...this.'

To Amber's alarm, the old man began to cough so violently that he slipped sideways in his chair and seemed incapable of struggling up again. In a flash, Jake had lunged forward and carefully eased Vincente upright before Amber could even move. She poured Vincente a fruit drink while a grim-faced Jake adjusted the blanket.

For a moment or two she hovered by Vincente's side, in case he needed anything else. His eyes were closed and he looked very pale. 'Should we call Jemima?' she whispered to Jake.

He had already lifted one of the thin, bony wrists and was checking Vincente's pulse. 'He'll be all right in a moment.'

They stood together, watching the huddled figure anxiously. It occurred to Amber that Jake had shown some human concern for Vincente. 'You don't hate him, do you?' she asked hopefully under her breath.

'You know what he did to my sister and her child,' Jake replied harshly. 'What do you think?'

Upset, she caught his arm. 'Give him a chance to explain—'

'I won't believe his lies. And don't ask me to like him!' Jake said through his teeth.

'He's ill—'

'And that automatically wipes away his sins?'

Amber cringed at Jake's bitter expression. 'No,' she said shakily. 'But he deserves a chance—'

'My sister had no chance. Even Vincente's wife preferred the terror of the outside world to the hell of living with him! Doesn't that tell you everything about the kind of man he was? Pascal hates him. Susannah hates him—'

'Quarrelling?' muttered Vincente maliciously.

Jake snatched in an angry breath. 'No!' he growled. 'Our marriage is solid. We love each other. You won't part us, however hard you try!'

Trembling, Amber tried to judge whether Jake was concerned for his marriage or the success of his planned revenge.

'Did he know who you were before he married you?' Vincente asked her slyly.

She felt weak. The life seemed to be draining from her body. *Did he?* If so... 'I—I don't know,' she whispered, asking Jake that question with her eyes.

His fingers tightened on her arm like a vice. 'Trust me!'

'When did you know?' she demanded. 'When?'

'Amber!' he ordered. 'Don't look at me like that.'

'How should I look?' she asked bitterly. 'Adoring? As if I'm in love with you? Is that what you've been working towards, Jake?'

'I care for you,' he growled. 'I love you. As you well know.'

'No, I don't know,' she said piteously. 'If I'm Vincente's daughter, then you stand to gain so much.'

She stopped to think, and recalled how furious Jake had been when he'd confronted her with the possibility that Leo had fathered her child. Now she knew why. It would have ruined Jake's vengeance.

'It's the ultimate revenge on Vincente that your child—*your* child,' she said jerkily, with a meaningful glance at his cold, brittle face, 'will inherit this plantation. Isn't that true?'

'Yes,' Jake said tightly. 'I can't deny that I find that a very satisfying and proper justice.'

Amber gave a low moan. She remembered something that Jake had said a while ago—something to the effect that it would be hard telling your child that its father was a liar, a cheat and an adulterer, who didn't think twice about breaking his marriage vows. Her stomach

felt hollow with shame. Jake might have been talking
about Vincente.

Jake had made her a pawn in a deadly serious game
of revenge. He'd recognised her vulnerability and played
on her weak state of mind. The memory of his words
brought tears to her eyes. Gently...slowly... Oh, yes,
she thought angrily, he'd made darn sure that he went
one careful step at a time, filling her head with dreams
which he had no intention of fulfilling.

A sick feeling settled in her stomach. Not the baby
this time but disappointment—the smashing of a dream.
He'd betrayed her. And she'd been used. Her lower lip
wobbled but her eyes flashed with anger. He wouldn't
get what he wanted. She'd see to that.

Jake had handed Vincente a letter. The old man
glanced at the writing on the front and tore the envelope
open. For a while there was an electric silence and then
Amber noticed that Vincente had gone a ghastly grey
colour and was swearing at Jake, calling him all the
names under the sun.

Vincente broke off when he saw Amber's shocked expression. 'Leave me,' he whispered. 'I need a little time
alone. Walk in the garden. Anything...'

Cold to the bone, Amber moved away, waiting till they
were a decent distance from the huddled figure. 'What
have you done, Jake?' she stormed. 'Have you no pity?'

'For him? No,' muttered Jake.

She glared. 'I respected you,' she said in a low voice.
'I thought you were a man of great kindness and integrity—'

'Amber! Don't doubt me!'

'What was that letter?' she demanded.

'Proof. I wouldn't have dreamed of meeting Vincente
without it.' A little more gently he said, 'I asked Mary

Brandon to write the letter to confirm the story I told you.'

Amber froze. In slow accusation her baleful eyes lifted to his. 'My...mother?' she said jerkily, hardly able to speak for fury. 'You've known who she is—*where* she is...all this time?'

'It was Mary who told me everything that had happened,' he said quietly. 'Not Stuart—though he filled in a few details. I told *him* what I knew. He wanted me to keep my mouth shut but my conscience wouldn't allow me to do that.'

Amber swallowed. 'She's alive, you've met her—and you have waited till *now* to tell me? You callous brute! You calculating, heartless devil! Jake, how could you do this to me—to anyone? How could you string me along, play me like some damn instrument—coaxing, wheedling, seducing, *lying*—?'

'You've met your mother, Amber,' he said huskily.

Her heart lurched. Feeling faint, she leant against a tree. 'I—I've met her? In Scotland?' Frantically she racked her brains. No elegant, cool blonde came to mind. 'Where? Who—?'

'Mary,' he said, watching her anxiously. 'Mary Smith, the woman who runs Unite, who became your friend and your mentor.'

'*Mary!*'

Amber gave a low cry and found herself falling. Jake flung his arms around her, easing her unresisting body to the ground so that she rested against the smooth bark of the tree.

'Take it easy, sweetheart.'

'Don't "sweetheart" me!' she said shakily. 'You're making it all up!' Her mouth dried. Now she remembered where she'd heard those three names being used together. 'Mary talked of her friends...' she went on. 'Sarah and Dot.'

'Yes. Three women who had a lot in common, who kept in touch and who helped one another. Sarah found it hard to cope with her child, who four years later was removed from her care. Dot and Mary subsequently got Sarah out of a women's refuge and they all set up home together. Gradually Mary was cured of her agoraphobia and went to work for Unite.'

'To—to help children find their parents,' Amber said, her voice cracking with the bitter irony.

Mary. The woman she admired above all others. And yet Mary had listened to all her confidences, wept a little when she'd told her about Stuart and Angus and Elizabeth, about the beauty of Castlestowe...and still she hadn't said who she was. Why? Amber raged. What harm would that have done? She'd told Jake, after all!

An immense feeling of rejection came down on her like a leaden weight. Mary didn't want her. And Jake didn't either. She was just a means to an end. An instrument of revenge for both of them.

'She told you. Not me,' she said bitterly.

'I was chatting to Mary during one long night in Mostar when we were under curfew,' Jake said quietly. 'She asked me if I had any connection with the Cavendish family who'd lived in St Lucia. When I said I had, the whole story came tumbling out. Some time later we met again and she said that Ginny was claiming to be Vincente's daughter.'

'How did she know?' Amber asked him sulkily.

'She'd never lost contact with Susannah,' he explained. 'Mary was annoyed—and kept saying that she wished someone could help you to gain your inheritance.'

'And when did she trace me?' she demanded.

'When you were at university and she gave you the job with Unite. But she couldn't bring herself to tell you that you'd been adopted—and that she was your mother.

It was obvious that you were very happy living in Castlestowe. She thought she ought not to disrupt your life. Then later, when you turned up in Africa and told us your mother had died, Mary realised you were at a crossroads. We talked about it and we both came to the same conclusion—that you ought to know of your adoption and that you should be given the opportunity to decide whether to trace your natural parents or not.'

'I should have been told everything,' she persisted. 'Mary could have come to me herself. Why didn't she?'

'Two reasons. One was Vincente,' replied Jake simply. 'She didn't want him to know where she was. And she was afraid you'd hate her for abandoning you. That would have hurt her. She has grown to love you, Amber, and she didn't want to risk losing you a second time.'

Amber was silent for a moment. 'I don't know how I feel. It's such a shock . . .' Her huge eyes flicked up to his. 'Where do you come in?' she asked bitterly.

Jake dropped his gaze. 'Mary and I were worried about you when we learned you were pregnant and Enzo had walked out on you. I said I'd marry you and Mary was delighted. She asked me to guide you to Vincente when I judged you to be fit enough. I was to carefully leak out information, bit by bit, so you weren't too stressed out by all the revelations you'd have to contend with.' He spread his hands in a gesture of appeal. 'I tried to make it easy for you by not loading you with too many shocks at one time. I think it was the hardest thing I've ever done in my life.'

'She thought highly of your judgement,' Amber said with a waspish sting in her tone. 'Pity she didn't know how single-minded you can be where your own interests are concerned. It suited you to marry me! It was a gift, me being pregnant and the daughter of the man you hate!'

It had all been planned. Nothing had been an accident and he had lied about falling in love with her. The sky seemed to whirl around. Jake's face appeared, ghastly white and anxious, moving backwards and forwards in front of her blurred vision till it steadied again briefly. 'I feel awful,' she rasped, and passed out.

CHAPTER EIGHT

AMBER knew dimly that Jake had carried her back to the house. She feigned sleep as he and Jemima made arrangements to put her in one of the guest rooms.

Jake had betrayed her. All that rubbish about half loving her from the moment he'd met her had been just that—rubbish. It had been a golden opportunity and he'd grabbed it with both hands.

Quite frighteningly calm, she assessed the situation. He'd been so clever. By making sure that she didn't find out the truth till she'd fallen in love with him he'd thought he'd made his position as her husband impregnable.

She could walk out on him at once, of course. Ask for a divorce. But that would be too easy.

She lay stiff and cold for hours, even after Jake came up and quietly slid into bed beside her and tried to hold her stiff, unresponsive body. For a while he gently stroked her back and then turned over and went to sleep.

That annoyed her intensely! Jake wanted Beau Rivage. Well, she'd make sure he had no share in it.

As for Vincente... Amber squeezed her eyes shut tightly in an effort to blot him from her mind. Angus was her father, she told herself fiercely. Angus and Elizabeth had loved her, made her what she was. And Stuart had always been devoted to her too.

People came and went. She ignored them. Day and night seemed to fuse together. People muttered in low voices and talked about shock. Once she was aware of

Vincente, wheezing by her bed, crying. And a doctor, taking her pulse and blood pressure while Jake held her limp hand and stroked her forehead. That made her restless and Jake was asked to stop.

After a while she realised that Jake wasn't sleeping with her any more. And although she knew that she must get up and do something, take her life in her hands and show Jake that she could live without him, somehow she couldn't raise the energy.

The heat stifled her, despite the paddle-fans. Jake sat day after day fanning her, trying to feed her, sometimes falling asleep where he sat. And then she'd look at him, loving him, hating him, despairing that the pretence had come to an end, because it had been wonderful whilst she'd believed in it.

Sometimes she woke from a nightmarish dream to find Jake dabbing her brow with a cool cloth. Sometimes she heard him pacing up and down in the room next door and Jemima's entreaties to him to come and eat.

Then one day he began to talk to her in earnest.

'I know you can hear me,' he said quietly. 'I know you're afraid that I've deceived you. But I haven't. I love you, Amber. Talk to me, Amber! For God's sake, talk to me!'

She shut out whatever else he said. His pain hurt her but she wasn't going to give in. He was in a panic because his plan was failing, whereas she felt as though she'd been mortally wounded. He persisted. He talked of his love, how he'd been irrevocably drawn to her at their first meeting and how he'd tried not to get involved with her because of the dangers of his job.

Over and over again he said that he'd suppressed furious bouts of jealousy during her affair with Enzo—and how he'd realised then the extent of his love for her.

Amber turned her face to the wall. Quietly and patiently he said it all again. And she crawled out of bed weakly, spurning his help, to sit staring stonily out of the window.

The days dragged. She watched the gardeners cutting back the hibiscus and listened to the breeze in the bamboo. Jake appeared every day to tell her quietly that he loved her. Then he took to reading the daily newspapers to her and she tried not to soften to the sound of his melodious voice. How could she ever trust him?

Languid and wan, she lay in the tumbled chaos of her sheets one morning, listening to the sound of Jake's slow footsteps as he went downstairs to answer a telephone call. Something fluttered in her stomach. And again. As still as a statue, she held her breath and waited. The little butterfly movement came more strongly.

Tears coursed down her cheeks. Her hands nursed her stomach as she fell in love, helplessly, totally in love, with the child growing within her. This child would be loved. This child would know its mother. And she'd fight for the life she wanted her baby to lead, no matter who tried to stop her.

There was a footfall and her eyes swivelled to the doorway, where Jake was standing. He looked terrible and for a moment her heart turned over with concern for him.

'I want to leave,' she said decisively. 'I'm not intending to stay here a moment longer than necessary. And I don't want to acknowledge Vincente as my father—'

'You must!' insisted Jake.

'Must?' She bristled. 'I'm under no obligation!'

'You must acknowledge Vincente because he *is* your father and he doesn't have long to live,' he said with exasperation. 'Let the man rest in peace, Amber.'

'Why should you care whether he goes to his grave in peace or torment?' she cried with sudden passion.

'Because that's the proper thing for *you* to do,' he said wearily. 'My feelings don't come into it.'

'You've spent months plotting and planning to wreak your vengeance on him! You got *married* to get even!' she said in disgust. 'You said once you were obsessed with me. I don't think so,' she grated. 'You're obsessed with Vincente, with revenge!'

'What do you want me to feel for him? Compassion, because he's dying? We're all going to die! He snuffed out two lives because he was careless and threw a half-smoked cigar into dry undergrowth. I saw my parents change from vital, enthusiastic people to mere shadows with no purpose in life. He turned me into a wanderer without roots. Don't speak to me of compassion where Vincente's concerned.'

'Oh, Jake!' she said brokenly. 'He's destroyed you too. Destroyed the love between us—'

'No!' Jake strode forward and caught her shoulders. 'Don't say that.'

'He's turned you into a monster like him!' she sniffed. 'You used me to—'

'No. No, I didn't use you, my darling. Oh, God!' he groaned sinking down onto the edge of the bed. 'Listen to me, Amber—'

'I won't! You've talked me into enough corners—'

'This isn't a corner!' he said angrily. 'I've told you so many times ... How do I get it into your thick skull that I married you because I was madly in love with you? I knew we'd be happy together. I wanted to make love to you so many times but I held back as much as I could.'

'I know. Why did you do that?' she asked defiantly. 'I'm intrigued to know your explanation.'

Jake's eyes glittered at her obvious scepticism. 'I held back because I was worried,' he said tightly, 'that when you learnt the whole story you would think I had used sex to persuade you to do what I wanted. It wasn't like that, Amber!' he said passionately. 'Almost from the start I wanted to cherish you and your child and love you for ever. I saw you walking away from life because Enzo had hurt you. It suddenly dawned on me that I too had walked away from something I should have dealt with long ago, and that I wouldn't be happy till I faced up to Caroline's death and confronted Vincente.'

'But you delayed doing even that,' she said, stubbornly refusing to believe him. 'When we arrived you kept stalling and saying we needn't see Vincente. You didn't even want me to meet him.'

'I knew we had a chance of being very, very happy,' he said, his voice taut and strained, as if he was having difficulty keeping his emotions under control. 'All we needed was time. I wanted to gain your trust. Amber, you know how well our relationship developed when we were together. We both needed that time to get to know one another. I wanted you to fall in love with me. Of course I did. I also wanted you to be rested and relaxed before you met Vincente. My greatest fear was that you'd mistrust my motives. But I swear I thought I was helping you and Mary to find justice. Please believe me!'

She wanted to. So badly. 'How can I?' she mumbled.

'I don't want to avenge Caroline's death at the expense of our marriage,' he said huskily. 'I can prove that to you. Listen to me. Listen!' he said impatiently when

she turned her head away. His fingers ruthlessly drew
her chin back till she was forced to meet his fierce eyes.
'For years I burned to see Vincente in a living hell,' he
growled. 'I knew I could do nothing to achieve that so
I threw myself into my work. And then there came the
chance for me to achieve my greatest desire.'

'I was right!' she cried.

He gave a wry smile and looked at her with such tenderness that she trembled. 'I meant my desire to marry
you!'

'And... Vincente?' she asked shakily.

'My revenge on him is within my grasp,' he said softly.
'But by taking it I'd lose you. And that I could never
bear.' His mouth touched hers in a tantalisingly brief
kiss. 'I love you,' he said hoarsely. 'And because of that
I think we would be happier if we forgot all about Beau
Rivage, if we metaphorically shut the door on Vincente
and the plantation, on what happened to my sister and
my nephew... and went home.'

For a moment it didn't sink in. Her enormous eyes
stared back at him uncomprehendingly. 'Home?
Castlestowe?'

'Yes, my darling. Tell Vincente you don't want to
inherit.'

'Me or... my child?'

'Or our child,' he said gently. 'I want to be with you
more than anything else. Let's go home—'

'But... you hate Vincente...'

'Yes,' he said more grimly. 'And I'd like to see him
get his comeuppance. But he's not worth the price. My
revenge would come too dear.'

Her eyes closed in relief. Vincente wouldn't destroy
them both. His evil influence had been wiped away by
Jake's love. 'Jake!' she sniffed.

'Crying, darling? Hey!' he said with a shaky laugh. 'Don't; you should be happy!'

She smiled through her tears and found herself sinking beneath his long, slow kiss.

'Ahem!'

'Mmm?' murmured Jake against her mouth.

'I didn't say that,' she mumbled dreamily.

Together they turned, laughing. Amber's laughter died in her throat and fresh tears filled her eyes. 'Mary!' she said, holding out her arms to the tall, grey-haired woman in the doorway. 'Oh, Mary!' And she was enfolded in Mary's arms. Her mother. She clung to her tightly, pouring out the love in her heart till she was gently pushed away.

Mary turned to Jake and half hugged the breath from him. 'Thank you!' she said huskily.

He grinned at her. 'Thank *you* for coming. You said you never would. I know how hard this must be for you. I'm grateful.'

'I had to get you off my back! You've pestered the life out of me these last few days,' said Mary ruefully. 'He's been out of his mind with worry about you, Amber. He said you'd taken it badly.' She laughed. 'Judging by what I saw when I walked in, I think you feel better now, don't you? No. Don't blush. You're lucky to have found a man who loves you as much as Jake does. He bent my ear about you often enough!'

'I wish you'd told me,' said Amber fervently. 'About Jake and how he felt. About being my m-mother...'

Mary squeezed her hand. 'Darling, I was scared. Particularly about losing your respect before Jake had time to pave the way. But also because I'd lied about Vincente. I—' she looked shamefaced '—I didn't want to face him.'

Jake frowned. 'Lied?'

'Look, I have to be frank,' she replied. 'Both Vincente and I were to blame for our marriage breakdown. I can't have been easy to live with,' she confessed. 'I suffered from agoraphobia and I wouldn't go out. Then when Pascal was six we had an argument because I felt he ought to know that he wasn't our son. Vincente disagreed.'

Amber thought of her own promise to Jake about her baby and felt upset. 'Vincente was violent, I gather. He had no right to treat you badly,' she said, showing Mary that she understood the situation and didn't condemn her.

'That's not true.' Mary took a deep breath. 'During the quarrel we yelled at each other and he tried to calm me down. Pascal thought Vincente was hurting me. I— I'm ashamed to say that when I ran away I used that as an excuse to justify leaving my husband. I elaborated on the truth. We made a mess of our lives, both of us.'

Amber looked at Jake. He seemed to be struggling with the fact that Vincente hadn't abused his wife after all.

'You told me he brought his mistress into this house,' he stated flatly.

Mary hung her head. 'That was the main reason I went. He told me at the time that she was a companion for me, because I was trapped in the house, but I didn't believe him—she wasn't particularly attractive but she was young and I'd hear them talking together some-times and put two and two together and made fifteen. He'd had mistresses before, you see. Our marriage had become a sham. I couldn't bear it any longer.

'She wasn't his mistress,' Mary confessed. 'I was wrong. Vincente has convinced me.'

'You would have left him anyway,' Amber said sympathetically.

'Yes...' Mary sighed. 'My pregnancy had decided me. I didn't want my child growing up to be Vincente's heir. So I took from him what he wanted most. You, Amber.' She bit her lip in remorse. 'I lost you too, of course. I was ill and bewildered and scared, too distraught to take responsibility for a young infant. But I paid for my selfishness over and over. I've regretted leaving you for every one of those twenty-five years of your life.'

'You weren't well...and I had a very happy upbringing,' said Amber, misty-eyed, longing to find the right words to comfort Mary.

Her mother tenderly touched her hand and their fingers linked. 'I know. I'm so grateful for that.'

'Have you and Vincente come to terms with one another now?' Amber asked hesitantly.

'I think so. We wish we'd talked and sorted it out long ago. We were both at fault, you see.'

'You're generous, Mary. I, however, can't forgive him,' Jake growled.

Mary gave him a look of great compassion. 'Because of Caroline? Oh, my dear, Susannah hasn't told you everything, has she? All these years she'd known the truth. You know that Vincente's cousin Louis seduced Susannah when she was fifteen?'

'Yes,' said Jake guardedly as Amber's eyes widened.

'They weren't married, of course—Susannah was too young,' went on Mary. 'Vincente flatly refused permission for any marriage to take place.' She smiled wanly. 'Louis and Vincente had been rivals. You see, I was engaged to Louis before Vincente swept me off my feet.'

'I know that,' said Jake.

'But you don't know what Susannah's only just told me.' Mary took a deep breath. 'Steel yourself, Jake. It was Louis who accidentally set fire to Pascal's house.'

'*Louis?*' exclaimed Jake in astonishment.

'Louis,' repeated Mary firmly. 'He'd been visiting Caroline and baby Charles. He paused to smoke a cigar outside the house and thought he'd extinguished it. We all know from what happened that he hadn't. And when Louis heard that the house had burnt down he told Susannah what he'd done and then killed himself in grief. Susannah has admitted that she deliberately blamed the fire and Louis's death on Vincente to blacken his name.'

'Oh, hell!' groaned Jake.

'I'm afraid we've all behaved rather badly,' said Mary contritely. 'And you two have been caught up in our human failings. Susannah wants to ask your forgiveness. She's beside herself with grief. I'm sorry you've both been hurt. That's why I came—to tell the truth.'

Jake sat quite still when Mary's voice had died away into the tense silence. And then he rose and began to pace up and down. Amber watched with pity in her heart as he came to terms with the fact that he'd spent years of his life hating an innocent man.

After a while, as Jake stood struggling with the truth, she slipped from the bed and put her arms around him. 'It's all right,' she soothed. 'Everything's fine now.'

'It's been such a shock!' he muttered. 'I must go to Vincente,' he added distractedly. 'Apologise.'

'Yes. In a little while,' she said softly. 'We must gather everyone together. The three of us, Vincente, Susannah, Pascal and Mandy, Leo and Ginny... Everyone must come and everyone will be reunited—even if it means that I have to stand up on a chair and go through the whole story till everyone's satisfied!' she added with a rueful laugh.

'And then we'll go home,' Jake said softly.

'Home!' she sighed. 'Will Vincente be very upset if we go?' she asked anxiously.

'Oh, Amber!' Jake said, ruffling her hair affectionately. 'You will always worry about people! I told him I thought you probably wouldn't stay and he said he understands. He knows you love Castlestowe and that your ties are stronger there. He is content to have found you.'

'He loves Ginny. She cares for him. She'll look after him, won't she?'

'I'm sure she will,' Jake assured her warmly.

'You know, Amber, you've brought us all together and healed old wounds,' came Mary's tearful voice.

Jake smiled and held out a welcoming arm so that all three of them were encircled in each other's arms. Then, after a moment, Mary kissed him on the cheek and discreetly left the room.

Amber's heart felt as if it was overflowing with love and tears and emotion. Dazed, elated, she and Jake held one another for a while and then went to talk to a deeply moved Vincente. A contrite Susannah suggested tentatively that Leo and Ginny should inherit Beau Rivage since Pascal was happy enough with his own plantation. To Susannah's delight, Vincente nodded and held out his arms to his estranged sister.

Amber sighed with pleasure. Soon, in perhaps a week or two, after she'd spent some time with Vincente and the others, she and Jake and Mary would be going home. Home. To Castlestowe—and Stuart—dear, devoted Stuart, who'd done more for her than she'd ever known.

'Oh, Jake!' she cried later that night, when they were kissing beneath the shower. 'My baby! Feel...'

'Oh, God!' he whispered, and gently knelt to kiss the smooth roundness of her stomach. 'Our baby.' He stood up smiling, turned off the shower and held her tight. 'We must be honest with our child. Not keep anything back.'

'I agree. We'll tell him or her the truth. We can do it tactfully. We needn't do a character assassination on Enzo. I don't think there'll be a problem. Parents are the people who love you,' she said softly, thinking of the two people who'd brought her up as their daughter.

'I want to know our child. I want to be with you as much as possible,' Jake said, his voice muffled in her neck. When he looked at her she could see that his eyes were moist with tears. 'I'll go in for another kind of war-reporting,' he said huskily, kissing her softly on the mouth. 'European politics. Yes?'

Amber laughed then wound her arms around his neck and dreamed—of her children on the moors, of Jake striding beside her, perhaps as they hurried to the castle for tea with Stuart and Mary. Of occasional meetings with Mandy and Pascal and their children, with Ginny and Leo and their family. She was happy. Truly, deeply happy, most of all because she was going to share her beloved home with the man she loved more than anything—even Castlestowe itself.

New York Times bestselling author

JANET DAILEY

delivers a touching new story
that will reawaken the magic
of Christmas in all of us!

SCROOGE WORE SPURS

Some people said Eben MacCallister was a scrooge.

But this hardened bachelor is about to be put to the test
when fate delivers four young children to his ranch one
December night and the only person willing to help is
his former fiancée...who hopes that the kids will
actually teach Eben a thing or two!

Available at your favorite retail outlet in
December 1997—only from MIRA® Books.

MIRA
BOOKS

The Brightest Stars in Women's Fiction.™

Look us up on-line at: http://www.romance.net　　MJD293

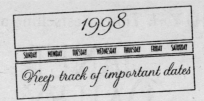

1998

SUNDAY MONDAY TUESDAY WEDNESDAY THURSDAY FRIDAY SATURDAY

Keep track of important dates

Three beautiful and colorful calendars that celebrate some of the most popular trends in America today.

Look for:

Just Babies—a 16 month calendar that features a full year of absolutely adorable babies!

1998 CALENDAR

Just Babies

16 months of adorable bundles of joy!

Hometown Quilts

1998 Calendar

A 16 month quilting extravaganza!

Hometown Quilts—a 16 month calendar featuring quilted art squares, plus a short history on twelve different quilt patterns.

Inspirations—a 16 month calendar with inspiring pictures and quotations.

Inspirations

A 16 month calendar that will lift your spirits and gladden your heart

Steeple Hill™

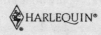

HARLEQUIN®

Value priced at $9.99 U.S./$11.99 CAN., these calendars make a perfect gift!

Available in retail outlets in August 1997.   CAL98

**Don't miss these Harlequin favorites
by some of our bestselling authors! Act now and
receive a discount by ordering two or more titles!**

HT#25720	A NIGHT TO REMEMBER	$3.50 U.S.	☐
	by Gina Wilkins	$3.99 CAN.	
HT#25722	CHANGE OF HEART	$3.50 U.S.	☐
	by Janice Kaiser	$3.99 CAN.	
HP#11797	A WOMAN OF PASSION	$3.50 U.S.	☐
	by Anne Mather	$3.99 CAN.	
HP#11863	ONE-MAN WOMAN	$3.50 U.S.	☐
	by Carole Mortimer	$3.99 CAN.	
HR#03356	BACHELOR'S FAMILY	$2.99 U.S.	☐
	by Jessica Steele	$3.50 CAN.	
HR#03441	RUNAWAY HONEYMOON	$3.25 U.S.	☐
	by Ruth Jean Dale	$3.75 CAN.	
HS#70715	BAREFOOT IN THE GRASS	$3.99 U.S.	☐
	by Judith Arnold	$4.50 CAN.	
HS#70729	ANOTHER MAN'S CHILD	$3.99 U.S.	☐
	by Tara Taylor Quinn	$4.50 CAN.	
HI#22361	LUCKY DEVIL	$3.75 U.S.	☐
	by Patricia Rosemoor	$4.25 CAN.	
HI#22379	PASSION IN THE FIRST DEGREE	$3.75 U.S.	☐
	by Carla Cassidy	$4.25 CAN.	
HAR#16638	LIKE FATHER, LIKE SON	$3.75 U.S.	☐
	by Mollie Molay	$4.25 CAN.	
HAR#16663	ADAM'S KISS	$3.75 U.S.	☐
	by Mindy Neff	$4.25 CAN.	
HH#28937	GABRIEL'S LADY	$4.99 U.S.	☐
	by Ana Seymour	$5.99 CAN.	
HH#28941	GIFT OF THE HEART	$4.99 U.S.	☐
	by Miranda Jarrett	$5.99 CAN.	

(limited quantities available on certain titles)

TOTAL AMOUNT	$	_____
DEDUCT: **10% DISCOUNT FOR 2+ BOOKS**	$	_____
POSTAGE & HANDLING	$	_____
($1.00 for one book, 50¢ for each additional)		
APPLICABLE TAXES*	$	_____
TOTAL PAYABLE	$	_____

(check or money order—please do not send cash)

To order, complete this form and send it, along with a check or money order for the
total above, payable to Harlequin Books, to: **In the U.S.:** 3010 Walden Avenue, P.O. Box
9047, Buffalo, NY 14269-9047; **In Canada:** P.O. Box 613, Fort Erie, Ontario, L2A 5X3.

Name: _____

Address: _____ City: _____

State/Prov.: _____ Zip/Postal Code: _____

*New York residents remit applicable sales taxes.
Canadian residents remit applicable GST and provincial taxes.

Look us up on-line at: http://www.romance.net   HBKOD97

HARLEQUIN PRESENTS®

It may be cold outside—but inside a
Harlequin Presents, the temperature's always
rising! Get under the covers of these sizzling
books from some of our hottest authors:

November 1997—**Gold Ring of Betrayal** (#1917)
Michelle Reid

Winner of the *Romantic Times* Reviewers' Choice
Award for best Harlequin Presents 1994-95

December 1997—**Merry Christmas** (#1923)
Emma Darcy

Presents bestselling author with over
50 million books in print

January 1998—**A Marriage to Remember** (#1929)
Carole Mortimer

"Carole Mortimer delivers quality romance."
—*Romantic Times*

Warm up this winter with Harlequin Presents!

Available wherever Harlequin books are sold.

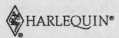 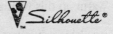